PENGUIN CLASSICS
A Man's Head

'I love reading Simeno   — William Faulkner

'A truly wonderful writer . . . marvellously readable – lucid,
simple, absolutely in tune with the world he creates'
— Muriel Spark

'Few writers have ever conveyed with such a sure touch, the
bleakness of human life'   — A. N. Wilson

'One of the greatest writers of the twentieth century . . .
Simenon was unequalled at making us look inside, though the
ability was masked by his brilliance at absorbing us obsessively
in his stories'   — *Guardian*

'A novelist who entered his fictional world as if he were part
of it'   — Peter Ackroyd

'The greatest of all, the most genuine novelist we have had in
literature'   — André Gide

'Superb . . . The most addictive of writers . . . A unique teller
of tales'   — *Observer*

'The mysteries of the human personality are revealed in all
their disconcerting complexity'   — Anita Brookner

'A writer who, more than any other crime novelist, combined
a high literary reputation with popular appeal'   — P. D. James

'A supreme writer . . . Unforgettable vividness' — *Independent*

'Compelling, remorseless, brilliant'   — John Gray

'Extraordinary masterpieces of the twentieth century'
— John Banville

GEORGES SIMENON

A Man's Head

Translated by DAVID COWARD

PENGUIN BOOKS

PENGUIN CLASSICS

Published by the Penguin Group
Penguin Books Ltd, 80 Strand, London WC2R ORL, England
Penguin Group (USA) Inc., 375 Hudson Street, New York, New York 10014, USA
Penguin Group (Canada), 90 Eglinton Avenue East, Suite 700, Toronto, Ontario, Canada M4P 2Y3
(a division of Pearson Penguin Canada Inc.)
Penguin Ireland, 25 St Stephen's Green, Dublin 2, Ireland (a division of Penguin Books Ltd)
Penguin Group (Australia), 707 Collins Street, Melbourne, Victoria 3008, Australia
(a division of Pearson Australia Group Pty Ltd)
Penguin Books India Pvt Ltd, 11 Community Centre, Panchsheel Park, New Delhi – 110 017, India
Penguin Group (NZ), 67 Apollo Drive, Rosedale, Auckland 0632, New Zealand
(a division of Pearson New Zealand Ltd)
Penguin Books (South Africa) (Pty) Ltd, Block D, Rosebank Office Park, 181 Jan Smuts Avenue,
Parktown North, Gauteng 2193, South Africa

Penguin Books Ltd, Registered Offices: 80 Strand, London WC2R ORL, England

www.penguin.com

First published in French as *La tête d'un homme* by Fayard 1931
This translation first published in Penguin Books 2014

013

Copyright 1931 by Georges Simenon Limited
Translation copyright © David Coward, 2014
GEORGES SIMENON ® Simenon.tm
MAIGRET ® Georges Simenon Limited
All rights reserved

The moral rights of the author and translator have been asserted

Typeset in Dante MT Std by Palimpsest Book Production Ltd, Falkirk, Stirlingshire
Printed and bound in Great Britain by Clays Ltd, Elcograf S.p.A.

ISBN: 978-0-141-39351-3

www.greenpenguin.co.uk

Penguin Books is committed to a sustainable
future for our business, our readers and our planet.
This book is made from Forest Stewardship
Council™ certified paper.

MIX
Paper from
responsible sources
FSC
www.fsc.org   FSC™ C018179

Contents

1. Cell 11, High Surveillance

When a bell somewhere rang twice, the prisoner was sitting on his bunk with his two large hands clasped about his folded knees.

For the space of perhaps a minute he did not move, as if suspended in time; then with a sudden release of breath, he stretched his arms and legs and stood up in his cell, a huge man, ungainly, his head too big, his arms too long and his chest hollow.

His face was unreadable, expressing only numbness or perhaps a kind of inhuman indifference. Yet before he moved across to the door with the spyhole, now closed, he brandished a fist towards one of the walls.

On the other side of that wall was an identical cell, one of the cells on the Santé prison's High Surveillance wing.

In it, as in four other cells, was a convicted criminal waiting for either a stay of execution or the arrival of the solemn party of men who would come one night and wake him without saying a word.

Every day for five days, every hour, every minute, the other prisoner had groaned, at times in a low monotonous whimper, at others accompanied by screams, tears, howls of defiance.

Number 11 had never set eyes on him, knew nothing of

him. At most, judging by his voice, he could make a guess that his neighbour was young.

At this moment, the groaning was weary, mechanical, while in the eyes of the man who had just got to his feet there was a flash of hatred, and he clenched his large-knuckled fists.

From the corridor and passageways, from the exercise yards, from every part of the fortress that is the Santé prison, from the streets surrounding it, from Paris, no sound reached him.

Except for the moaning of the man in cell 10.

Number 11 pulled jerkily on his fingers, then froze twice before reaching out to put one hand on the door.

The cell light was on, as laid down in regulations for High Surveillance watch.

Normally, a guard was required to be on duty in the corridor, to open the doors of all five prisoners every hour.

Number 11's hands played around the lock with a gesture made solemn by a tremor of fear.

The door swung open. The guard's chair was there. No one was sitting on it.

The man began walking, very fast, bent double, his senses reeling. His face was dead white, and only the red-tinged lids of his greenish eyes had any colour.

Three times he stopped and went back the way he had come because he had taken a wrong turning and had come up against locked doors.

At the end of one corridor he heard voices. Guards were smoking and chatting in a duty room.

Finally he found himself in a yard, where the darkness

was punctured at intervals by the round discs of lamps. A hundred metres ahead, in front of the outer gate, a sentry was walking to and fro.

To one side was a lighted window through which a man could be seen, pipe in mouth, bent over a desk littered with papers.

Number 11 wished he could have taken another look at the note he had found three days earlier stuck to the bottom of his dinner pail, but he had chewed and swallowed it following the instructions of whoever had sent it. For while, only an hour before, he had known what it said by heart, there were now parts of it which he could not remember exactly.

At 2 a.m., 15 October, your cell door will be left open and the guard will be busy elsewhere. If you follow the directions as marked below . . .

The man passed a burning hand over his forehead, stared in terror at the discs of light and almost cried out loud when he heard footsteps. But they came from the other side of the wall, from the street. Free people were talking out there, and their heels clacked on the pavement.

'When I think they charge fifty francs a seat . . .'

It was a woman's voice.

'Yes, but they have expenses . . .' came a man's voice.

The prisoner felt his way along the wall, stopped because his foot had encountered a stone, listened, so whey-faced, cutting such an odd figure with those interminable arms which dangled loosely, that if this had been happening anywhere else people would just have assumed he was a drunk.

*

3

The small knot of men was waiting less than fifty metres from the invisible prisoner, in a recess of the wall, near a door on which was written: *Bursar's Office*.

Detective Chief Inspector Maigret had chosen not to lean against the blackened brick wall. With his hands thrust into the pockets of his overcoat, he was standing so squarely on his strong legs, so absolutely still, that he gave the impression of lifeless bulk.

But at regular intervals there came the dragging sizzle of his pipe. His eyes were watchful, but he couldn't quite eradicate the apprehension in them.

A dozen times at least, he must have nudged the shoulder of Coméliau, the examining magistrate, who would not stay where he had been put.

Coméliau had come directly from a social engagement in evening dress, his thin moustache neatly trimmed and with more colour in his cheeks than usual.

Close to them, with a scowl on his face and the collar of his coat turned up, stood Monsieur Gassier, governor of the Santé, who was trying to distance himself from what was happening.

There was a slight chill in the air. The sentry by the gate stamped his feet, and his breath rose in the air like thin columns of steam.

The prisoner, who avoided areas that were lit, could not be seen. But however careful he was to make no noise, he could still be heard moving around, and the onlookers were able, after a fashion, to follow his every movement.

After ten minutes, the examining magistrate shuffled nearer to Maigret and opened his mouth to say something.

But the inspector gripped his shoulder with such strength that the magistrate desisted, sighed and from a pocket mechanically took a cigarette, which was snatched from his hands.

All three had understood. Number 11 did not know the way and at any moment might stumble into a patrol.

And they could do nothing about it! They could hardly lead him by the hand to the place at the foot of the wall where the parcel of clothes had been left for him and where a knotted rope dangled.

At intervals a vehicle drove past in the street outside. Sometimes there were also people talking, and their voices echoed in a particular way in the prison yard.

All the three men could do was to exchange glances. The look in the governor's eyes was bad-tempered, sarcastic, fierce. Coméliau, the examining magistrate, was aware of his own growing anxiety, and the apprehension too.

Maigret alone did not flinch, his strength of will ensuring that he remained confident. But if he had been standing in a strong light, his brow would have been observed to glisten with sweat.

When the half-hour struck, the man was still dithering, all at sea. But one second later, the three watching men were all startled and felt the same shock.

They had not heard the release of breath, they had rather sensed it, they could feel the feverish haste of their man who had just stumbled over the parcel of clothes and seen the rope.

The footsteps of the sentry continued to mark the

rhythm of passing time. The magistrate took his opportunity and hissed:

'You're sure he . . . ?'

Maigret turned such a look on him that he fell silent. The rope twitched. They made out a lighter stain against the dark wall: the face of number 11, who was using his powerful wrists to haul himself up.

It took an age. It took ten, twenty times longer than they had anticipated. And when he reached the top, it looked as if he had given up, because he had completely stopped moving.

They could make him out now, or at least his silhouette, lying flat on the top of the wall.

Was he paralysed by vertigo? Was he hesitating about dropping down into the road? Were there passers-by or a courting couple crouching in some recess who were stopping him?

Coméliau snapped his fingers impatiently. The governor muttered:

'I don't suppose you need me any more . . .'

The rope was hauled up so that it could be dropped down the other side. The man disappeared.

'If I didn't have such confidence in you, detective chief inspector, I swear I'd never have let myself be mixed up in anything like this. All the same, I still think Heurtin is guilty. And what if he manages to get away from you? What then?'

'Will I see you tomorrow?' was all that Maigret asked.

'I'll be in my office any time after ten.'

They shook hands without saying anything more. The

governor held out a hand grudgingly and, as he left, muttered a few indistinct words.

Maigret remained close to the wall for a few moments longer and did not move off towards the gate until he had heard someone running off as fast as he could. He gave a wave to the guard on duty, looked up and down the empty street and walked along it and then into Rue Jean-Dolent.

'Did he get away?' he asked a dark figure which hugged the wall.

'Headed towards Boulevard Arago. Dufour and Janvier are on his tail.'

'You can go home now.'

Maigret, his mind elsewhere, shook the officer's hand, moved off with his stolid tread, head down, lighting his pipe as he went.

It was four in the morning when he pushed open the door of his office on Quai des Orfèvres. With a sigh he took off his overcoat, swallowed half the contents of a glass of warm beer which had been left among his papers and sat heavily into his chair.

In front of him was a fat manila file on which a police clerk had written in a flowery hand: *Heurtin Case*.

He waited for three hours. The bare electric bulb was surrounded by a cloud of smoke, which stirred at the slightest movement of air. From time to time, Maigret got up to poke the stove then returned to his seat but not before removing first his jacket, then his collar and finally his waistcoat.

The phone was within easy reach, and at around seven

o'clock he lifted the receiver just to make sure that they had not forgotten to give him an outside line.

The buff-coloured file was open. Reports, newspaper cuttings, witness-statements and photographs had spilled out on to the desk, and Maigret stared at them distantly, sometimes reaching for a document not so much to read it as to confirm a train of thought.

The whole collection was topped by a newspaper cutting with a forceful headline spread over two newspaper columns:

Joseph Heurtin, killer of Madame Henderson and her maid, sentenced to death this morning.

Maigret was smoking continuously, keeping an anxious eye on the telephone, which remained obstinately silent.

At ten past six, it rang, but it was a wrong number.

From where he sat, the inspector could read parts of various documents, though he now knew them by heart.

Joseph Jean-Marie Heurtin, 27, born Melun, a delivery man for Monsieur Gérardier, a florist in Rue de Sèvres . . .

The man's photograph was visible. It had been taken a year before in a fairground booth at Neuilly. A big man with unusually long arms, triangular-shaped head, washed-out complexion and clothes which denoted a vulgar dress sense.

Brutal Killing at Saint-Cloud
Rich American stabbed to death along with her maid

It had happened in July.

Maigret pushed away the gruesome shots from Criminal Records: both corpses, seen from different angles, blood everywhere, faces convulsed, night clothes disordered, stained, torn . . .

Detective Chief Inspector Maigret of the Police Judiciaire has cleared up the Saint-Cloud tragedy. The murderer is behind bars.

He ruffled through the papers spread out in front of him and found the cutting, which was dated ten days earlier:

Joseph Heurtin, killer of Madame Henderson and her maid, sentenced to death this morning . . .

In the courtyard of the Préfecture, a police van was disembarking the previous night's haul, who were mostly women. The first footsteps of the day could be heard in the corridors, and the mist above the Seine was dispersing.

'That you, Dufour?'

'Yes, sir.'

'Well?'

'Nothing . . . That is . . . If you want, I'll go down there myself . . . But for the moment, Janvier can manage on his own . . .'

'Where is he?'

'At the Citanguette.'

'Say again, the what?'

'A bistro, not far from Issy-les-Moulineaux. I'll get a taxi and join you so I can put you in the picture.'

Maigret paced up and down, sent out an office junior to order coffee and croissants for him at the Brasserie Dauphine.

He had just begun to eat when Inspector Dufour, a small man neatly turned out in his grey suit and very high, very stiff detachable collar, came in with his usual air of mystery.

'First thing: what's this Citanguette?' growled Maigret. 'Sit down.'

'A bistro used by boatmen on the bank of the Seine between Grenelle and Issy-les-Moulineaux.'

'Did he make straight for it?'

'Not at all. And it was a miracle he didn't manage to give Janvier and me the slip.'

'Have you had breakfast?'

'Yes, at the Citanguette.'

'Very well, tell me what happened.'

'You saw him get away, didn't you? At first he ran as if he was scared of being recaptured. He didn't stop being jittery until he got to the Lion de Belfort. He halted and stared at it. He seemed bewildered.'

'Did he know he was being tailed?'

'Definitely not! He never turned round once.'

'And then?'

'I think a blind man, or somebody who'd never been

to Paris before, would have behaved just as he did. He suddenly turned into the avenue that runs through Montparnasse cemetery. I forget what it's called. There wasn't a soul about. It was pretty gloomy just there. He couldn't have known where he was because when he walked through the iron gates and saw the tombstones he started running again.'

'Go on.'

Maigret, his mouth full, seemed more relaxed.

'We got to Montparnasse. The big cafés were closed, but a few clubs were still open. I remember that he stopped at one of them. There was the sound of jazz coming from inside. Then this little street-seller went up to him with her basket of flowers, and he ran off again.'

'Which way did he go?'

'No particular way, really. He went down Boulevard Raspail. Then he doubled back down a side street and came out again outside the entrance to Montparnasse station.'

'How did he seem?'

'He didn't seem like anything. The same as when he was being investigated, as when he was in court. Very pale. And a scared, unfocused look in his eyes. Half an hour later, we were at Les Halles.'

'And no one had tried to speak to him?'

'No one.'

'And did he post anything in a letterbox?'

'I'm positive he didn't. Janvier was following him on one side of the road, and I was on the other. We didn't miss a thing he did. Wait! He did stop for a moment at a stand selling hot sausages and fries. He hesitated and then he was off again, perhaps because he'd caught sight of a uniformed officer.'

'Did you get the impression he was looking for a particular address?'

'I didn't. You'd have thought he was a drunk who goes in whatever direction God points him. Then we were back at the Seine, at Place de la Concorde. He decided he was going to walk along the riverbank. He stopped and sat down two or three times.'

'Sat on what?'

'Once on the stone parapet and another time on a bench. I couldn't swear to it but I think the second time he was crying. Anyway, he was holding his head in both hands.'

'No one else on the bench?'

'Nobody. Then we walked some more. Imagine how far, all the way to Moulineaux! Now and then he'd stop and look down at the water. The tugs were beginning to move around. Then the factory workers started filling the streets. He still kept going, like a man who has no idea what he's going to do next.'

'Anything else?'

'That's about it. Oh, one thing. When he got to Pont Mirabeau, he put both hands in his pockets and took something out of them . . .'

'Five-franc notes.'

'That's what Janvier and I both thought we saw. At that point, he started looking round him for something. Obviously a bistro! But nothing was open on the Right Bank.

He crossed over. He went into a small bar full of stokers and ordered a coffee and a tot of rum.'

'The Citanguette?'

'Not yet. Janvier and I had legs like jelly. And unlike him we couldn't buy a drink to warm us up! Off he went again. He led us this way and that. Janvier, who took a note of all the streets, will give you a full report . . . In the end, we got back to the river, came out near a large factory. Down that way, it's pretty deserted.

'There are a few bushes and grass like in the country among all the heaps of spoil. Barges are moored up near a crane. Maybe twenty of them.

'The Citanguette is an inn you wouldn't expect to find there. A small bistro where they serve food. On the right is an extension with a mechanical piano and a sign saying: "Dancing Saturdays and Sundays".

'Our man drank another coffee and more rum. They brought him a plate of sausages after making him wait a long time for it. He spoke to the landlord, and a quarter of an hour later we saw them both disappear upstairs.

'When the landlord came back, I went in. I asked him point-blank if he had let any rooms.

'He said: "Why? Has *he* been up to something?"

'Clearly a man used to having dealings with the police. There was no point trying to bluff it out. I preferred to scare him. I told him that if he breathed one word to his customer, his place would be shut down.

'He doesn't know him, I'm sure of that. The clientele is mostly men from the barges, and, as soon as it's midday, the workers from the factory nearby all troop in for an aperitif.

'Apparently when Heurtin got inside his room, he threw himself on the bed without taking his shoes off. The landlord told him off, so he dropped them on the floor and immediately fell asleep.'

'Has Janvier stayed on?'

'He's still there. You can call him because the Citanguette has a telephone on account of the bargemen. They often need to get in touch with their owners.'

Maigret picked up the phone. A few moments later, Janvier was on the other end of the line.

'Hello? What's our man doing now?'

'Sleeping.'

'Anything suspicious to report?'

'Nothing. All quiet as quiet. You can hear him snoring from the foot of the stairs.'

Maigret hung up and ran his eyes over the small figure of Dufour from head to foot.

'You won't let him give you the slip?' he asked.

The officer was about to protest, but Maigret put one hand on his shoulder and went on in a sober voice:

'Listen, son. I know you'll do everything you can. But my job is on the line here! And a lot else besides. Fact is, I can't go myself. The wretch knows me.'

'Sir, I swear . . .'

'Don't swear, just go.'

And with a curt movement of his hand, Maigret swept the various documents into the manila folder, which he placed in a drawer.

'And if you need more men, don't hesitate to ask.'

Joseph Heurtin's picture was still on the desk, and

Maigret gazed briefly at his bony head, flapping ears and wide, bloodless lips.

Three medics had examined the man. Two had said:

Low intelligence. Fully responsible for his actions.

The third, quoted by the defence, had coyly ventured:

Troubled atavism. Diminished responsibility.

And Maigret, who had arrested Joseph Heurtin, had told the chief of police, the public prosecutor and the examining magistrate:

'He's either insane or innocent!'

And he had undertaken to prove it.

From the corridor came the receding sound of Inspector Dufour's footsteps as he went trippingly on his way.

2. The Sleeping Man

It was eleven o'clock when Maigret, after a brief meeting with Coméliau, the examining magistrate, who still did not feel fully reassured, arrived at Auteuil.

The weather was dull, the streets dirty and the sky sat low over the rooftops. On Maigret's side of the river was a line of affluent blocks of flats, while the bank opposite already had an industrial zone look to it: factories, patches of waste ground, unloading wharves littered with heaps of rubble.

Between these two townscapes flowed the Seine, grey, leaden and ruffled by the comings-and-goings of tug-boats.

The Citanguette was not hard to spot, even from a distance, an isolated structure in the middle of a piece of ground cluttered with all sorts of debris: piles of bricks, old rusting car chassis, scraps of roofing felt and even lengths of railway track.

A two-storey building, painted an ugly red, with an outside terrace with three tables and the traditional awning bearing the words: *Wines – Snacks*. Dockers emerged. They were clearly unloading cement because they were white from head to foot. At the door, as they left, they each shook hands with a man in a blue apron, the proprietor of the establishment, then headed off unhurriedly towards a barge moored at the quayside.

Maigret looked weary and dull-eyed, but the fact that

he had just spent a sleepless night was not the problem.

It was his habit to let himself droop like this, to wilt, every time he'd pursued a quarry relentlessly and finally had him within reach.

A reaction. He would feel sickened and did not try to fight it.

He noticed a hotel just opposite the Citanguette and walked up to reception.

'I'd like a room overlooking the river.'

'Monthly rate?'

He gave a shrug. He was not in the mood to be crossed.

'For as long as I want it! Police Judiciaire.'

'We don't have anything available.'

'Fine. Give me the register.'

'One moment . . . Wait! . . . I'll just phone the porter upstairs to make sure number 18 . . .'

'Cretin!' muttered Maigret between his teeth.

He was, of course, given the room. The hotel was luxurious. The porter asked:

'Any bags needing to be brought up?'

'No. Just bring me a pair of binoculars.'

'But . . . I don't know if . . .'

'Look, just go and get the binoculars from wherever you have to!'

He removed his overcoat with a sigh, opened the window and filled a pipe. Less than five minutes later, he was brought a pair of mother-of-pearl binoculars.

'These belong to the manager's wife. She says to be . . .'

'That's all! Now clear off! . . .'

*

By now he knew every last detail of the façade of the Citanguette. One upstairs window was open. Through it he could see an unmade bed with a vast red eiderdown lying sideways on it and a pair of carpet slippers on a sheepskin rug.

'The landlord's room!'

Next to it was another window, but this one was shut. Then a third which was open and framed a fat woman in a dressing gown who was doing her hair.

'The landlord's wife . . . Or maybe the maid.'

Downstairs, the landlord was wiping his tables with a cloth. At one of them, Inspector Dufour was sitting nursing a large glass of red wine.

The two men were talking, that much was obvious.

Further along, on the edge of the stone quayside, a young man with fair hair, wearing a mackintosh and a grey cap, appeared to be watching the cement being unloaded from the barge.

It was Inspector Janvier, one of the youngest officers in the Police Judiciaire.

In Maigret's room, at the head of the bed, was a phone. The inspector lifted the receiver.

'Reception?'

'You wanted something?'

'Connect me to the bistro on the other side of the river. It's called the Citanguette.'

'As you wish,' said a starchy voice.

It took some time. But eventually, from his window, Maigret saw the landlord put his cloth down and make for a door. Then the phone rang in his room.

'You're through to the number you asked for.'

'Hello? Is that the Citanguette? . . . Would you ask the customer who is there now, in your bar, to come to the phone . . . Yes! . . . There's no possible mistake since there's only one there . . .'

And through the window he saw the bewildered landlord speak to Dufour, who stepped into the booth.

'Listen . . .'

'Is that you, chief?'

'I'm across the river, in the hotel you can see from your table . . . What's our man doing?'

'He's asleep.'

'You've seen him?'

'A little while back I went up and listened outside his door . . . I could hear him snoring . . . So I opened the door a crack and I saw him . . . He's out cold, still in his clothes . . .'

'You're sure the landlord didn't tip him off?'

'He's too scared of the police! He's already been in trouble, some time back. He was threatened with having his licence taken away. So, he keeps his nose clean.'

'How many exits?'

'Two. The front door and another, which opens into a yard. Janvier's got that covered from his position.'

'Has anyone gone upstairs?'

'Nobody. And nobody can without passing me. The stairs are inside the bistro, behind the counter.'

'Good . . . Have your lunch there . . . I'll phone again later . . . Try to look like a barge-owner's agent.'

Maigret put the receiver down, dragged an armchair to

the open window, felt cold, fetched his overcoat from where it hung and put it on.

'Have you finished your call?' asked the hotel switchboard.

'Quite finished. I want you to send up some beer. And tobacco. Dark shag.'

'We don't keep tobacco.'

'Well, you'll just have to send out for some!'

At three in the afternoon, he was still in the same place, the binoculars on his knees, an empty glass within reach. A powerful smell of pipe-smoke filled the room, despite the open window.

He had dropped the morning papers on the floor. They carried the police statement:

Death Penalty Man Escapes from Santé Prison!

From time to time Maigret continued to shrug his shoulders, cross and uncross his legs.

At 3.30, he received a phone call from the Citanguette.

'Any developments?' he asked.

'No. He's still sleeping.'

'So?'

'Quai des Orfèvres have been on the line asking where you are. It seems that the examining magistrate needs to speak to you at once.'

This time, Maigret did not shrug his shoulders but spat a very blunt epithet, hung up and called the switchboard.

'Prosecutor's office, please. It's urgent.'

He knew exactly what Monsieur Coméliau would say!

'Ah! Is that you, detective chief inspector? At last! No one could tell me where you were. But at Quai des Orfèvres they informed me that you had men watching the Citanguette. I rang there . . .'

'What's happened?'

'First, do you have anything new?'

'Absolutely nothing. *Our man is asleep . . .*'

'Are you sure? . . . He hasn't escaped, has he?'

'If I exaggerated slightly, I'd say that at this very moment I can see him sleeping.'

'You know, I'm starting to regret that . . .'

' . . . that you listened to me? But the justice minister himself agreed it . . .'

'Yes, but wait a minute! The morning papers published your statement.'

'I saw it.'

'But have you seen the afternoon editions? . . . No? . . . Try to get hold of *Le Sifflet* . . . Yes. I know it's a scandal sheet . . . but even so! . . . Will you hang on for just a moment? . . . Hello? . . . Still there? I'll read it out . . . It's a short paragraph from *Le Sifflet* . . . It's headed "Reason of State" . . . Are you listening, Maigret? . . . Here it is:

This morning's papers published a semi-official statement revealing that Joseph Heurtin, sentenced to death by the Assize Court of the Seine District and held on High Surveillance at the Santé prison, had escaped in baffling circumstances.

We can add that these circumstances are not baffling for everybody.

In fact, Joseph Heurtin did not escape. He was made to escape. And it happened on the eve of the date fixed for his execution.

We are still unable to give details of the appalling charade which was played out last night at the Santé, but we can confirm that it was the police, with the collusion of the courts, who oversaw this faked escape.

Does Joseph Heurtin know?

If he doesn't, we cannot find words to describe this operation, which is probably unique in the annals of crime.

Maigret had listened to every last word without moving a muscle. At the other end of the line, the voice of the examining judge faltered.

'Well? What do you have to say?'

'That it proves I'm right. *Le Sifflet* didn't get hold of the story by itself. Nor was it one of the six prison and police officers in the know who gave the game away. It's . . .'

'It's . . . ?'

'I'll tell you that this evening! So far so good, Monsieur Coméliau!'

'You really think so? And what if the other papers take up the story?'

'There'll be a scandal.'

'You see . . .'

'And is a man's head not worth a touch of scandal?'

Five minutes later he was on the phone to the Préfecture.

'Sergeant Lucas? . . . Listen, I want you to go round to

the editorial office of *Le Sifflet*. It's in Rue Montmartre. Have a quiet word with the man in charge. Put the squeeze on him. We must know where he got his information about the escape from the Santé . . . I'll bet my bottom dollar that he got a letter this morning, or a pneumatic note . . . I want you to get your hands on it and bring it here . . . Got that?'

The operator asked:

'Have you finished, caller?'

'No, mademoiselle. Pass me back to the Citanguette.'

Moments later, Inspector Dufour was reporting:

'He's sleeping. A while back I stayed with my ear glued to his door for a quarter of an hour. I heard him talking in his sleep; a nightmare it was, calling for his mother!'

Training his binoculars on the closed window on the first floor of the Citanguette, Maigret could imagine the sleeping man as clearly as if he had been sitting at his bedside.

Yet he had met him for the first time only in July on the day, barely forty-eight hours after the murder at Saint-Cloud, he had laid one hand on his shoulder and muttered:

'Don't kick up a fuss. Just come with me . . .'

They were in Rue Monsieur-le-Prince, in a nondescript building where Joseph Heurtin had a room on the sixth floor.

The woman in the concierge's lodge said:

'He was steady, quiet, hard-working . . . Except that sometimes he seemed a bit odd . . .'

'Did he ever have callers?'

'No. And, except just recently, he never got home after midnight.'

'And recently?'

'He got back later two or three times. Once, last Wednesday, he rang for me to open the front door. Just before four in the morning, it was.'

That Wednesday was the day the murder had been committed at Saint-Cloud. The pathologists gave the time of death of both women as around 2 a.m.

But didn't they already have formal proof that Heurtin was guilty? The evidence had been gathered by Maigret himself.

The villa was located on the Saint-Germain road, less than a kilometre from the Pavillon Bleu. Now, Heurtin walked into this establishment at midnight. He was alone. He drank four grogs one after another. As he paid, he dropped a train ticket from his pocket, single, third class, Paris to Saint-Cloud.

Mrs Henderson, the widow of an American diplomat with connections to one of the great banking families, lived by herself in the villa. Since the death of her husband, there was no one on the ground floor.

She had only one servant, more companion than maid, Élise Chatrier, who was French and had spent her childhood in England and been given an excellent education.

Twice a week, a gardener came from Saint-Cloud to attend to the modest grounds which surrounded the villa.

Few visitors. From time to time, William Crosby, the old lady's nephew, called with his wife.

Now, on that July night – it was the 7th – cars were driving past as usual along the main road to Deauville.

At 1 a.m. the Pavillon Bleu and the other restaurants and supper-clubs closed their doors.

A motorist subsequently stated that around 2.30 a.m. he had seen a light on the first floor of the villa and shadows moving about oddly.

At six, the gardener arrived. It was his day. He usually opened the gate at eight, without making any noise. Élise Chatrier would call him in and give him his breakfast.

But at eight, he could hear nothing. At nine, the villa's doors were still not open. He felt anxious, knocked and, when there was no reply, he went off and alerted the police officer on duty at the nearest crossroads.

Soon after, the crime was discovered. In Mrs Henderson's room, the body of the old lady was lying across the hearthrug, her nightdress all bloodied. She had been stabbed a dozen times in the chest with a knife.

Élise Chatrier had experienced the same fate in the room next door, where she slept at the request of her employer, who was afraid of being taken ill in the night.

A brutal double murder, the kind the police call a cold, callous crime in all its horror.

And evidence everywhere: footprints, traces of bloody fingers on the curtains . . .

There were the usual formalities: arrival of the prosecutor's people, a visit from Criminal Records, multiple tests, autopsies . . .

It fell to Maigret to lead the police investigation, and it took him less than two days to get on Heurtin's trail.

It was so clearly signposted! In the corridors of the villa there were no carpets, and the wooden floors were kept polished.

A few photographs were enough to produce footprints of exceptional clarity.

They were of shoes with brand-new rubber soles. In order to prevent them slipping when it rained, the rubber was ribbed in a distinctive pattern and, in the middle of each, the maker's name was still clearly legible together with an order number.

A few hours later, Maigret walked into a shoe shop on Boulevard Raspail and learned that just one pair of shoes in that style and size – a 44 – had been sold during the preceding few weeks.

'I've got it! It was a delivery man. He turned up with his three-wheel carrier. We often see him hereabouts.'

Another few hours later and the inspector had questioned Monsieur Gérardier, the florist in Rue de Sèvres, and found the famous shoes on the feet of his delivery man, Joseph Heurtin.

All that remained was to compare fingerprints. This was done in the labs of Criminal Records in the Palais de Justice.

The experts, instruments in hand, pored over them, and their conclusion was instantaneous:

'That's our man!'

'Why did you do it?'
   'I never killed anybody!'
   'Who gave you Madame Henderson's address?'

'I never killed anybody!'

'What were you doing in her villa at two in the morning?'

'I don't know!'

'How did you get back from Saint-Cloud?'

'I never got back from Saint-Cloud.'

He had a large head, pallid and horribly battered. And his eyelids were red like those of a man who has not slept for several nights.

In his room in Rue Monsieur-le-Prince, a search discovered a bloodstained handkerchief. Tests showed that it was human blood and even found bacilli in it which matched those in the blood of Mrs Henderson.

'I never killed anybody!'

'Who do you want for a lawyer?'

'I don't want a lawyer.'

The court assigned one to him, a brief named Joly, who was only thirty and out of his depth.

The police psychiatrists kept Heurtin under observation for seven days then reported:

'He's not a degenerate! The man is responsible for his actions, despite his current depressed state, which is the result of a violent nervous shock to the system.'

Then it was the holiday period. Another investigation called Maigret away to Deauville. In the view of Coméliau, the examining magistrate, the case was straightforward, and a ruling from the prosecution service confirmed his opinion.

And this despite the fact that Heurtin had not stolen anything and had no apparent reason for wanting the deaths of Mrs Henderson and her maid.

Maigret had traced his past as far back as he could. He got to know the man in both mind and body at every stage of his life.

He was born at Melun, where his father was a waiter at the Hôtel de la Seine and his mother a laundress.

Three years later, his parents were running a bistro not far from Melun prison. They did not make a go of it and moved to an inn at Nandy, in the Seine-et-Marne department.

Joseph Heurtin was six when he acquired a sister, Odette.

Maigret had a picture of him, in a sailor suit, crouching by a bearskin on which the baby, arms and legs in the air, was lying.

At thirteen, Heurtin was looking after the horses and helping his father to serve the customers.

At seventeen, he was a waiter at Fontainebleau, in a smart hotel.

At twenty-one, after finishing his military service, he arrived in Paris, found somewhere to live in Rue Monsieur-le-Prince and was taken on by Monsieur Gérardier as a delivery man.

'He used to read a lot,' said Monsieur Gérardier.

'His only entertainment was going to the cinema,' said his landlady.

But there was no visible connection between him and the villa at Saint-Cloud!

'Had you ever been to Saint-Cloud before?'

'Never!'

'What did you do on Sundays?'

'I used to read.'

Mrs Henderson was not a customer of the florist. Nothing singled out her villa enough to attract a visit from a burglar more than any other. In any case, nothing had been stolen.

'Why don't you talk?'

'I got nothing to say.'

For a whole month, Maigret had been detained at Deauville, where he had hunted down a gang of international swindlers.

In September, he had visited Heurtin in his cell at the Santé. He had found a shadow of the man.

'I don't know anything! I never killed anybody!'

'But you were at Saint-Cloud . . .'

'I want to be left alone.'

'A run-of-the-mill case!' was the opinion of the prosecutor's office. 'It will keep for the autumn.'

And on 1 October, Heurtin opened the autumn session of the Assizes.

Joly, his counsel, had come up with a single defence tactic: to ask for a new examination of the mental state of his client. The doctor he had chosen had told the court:

'Diminished responsibility . . .'

To which the reply from the prosecution was:

'This was a cold, callous and appalling crime! If Heurtin didn't steal anything, it was because he was prevented from doing so by some circumstance or other. All told, he struck his victims eighteen times with a knife!'

Photographs of the victims had been handed round the members of the jury, who pushed them away with disgust.

'GUILTY', on all counts.

Death! The next day, Joseph Heurtin was transferred to the top-security block with four other men who had also been sentenced to death.

'Isn't there anything you want to tell me?' Maigret made a point of coming to ask him, for he was not happy with himself.

'No.'

'You do know you're going to be executed?'

Heurtin wept, still as pale as ever, his eyes red.

'Who was in this with you?'

'Nobody.'

Maigret returned every day, even though officially he had no business looking into the case any further.

And every morning he found Heurtin more and more crushed but calm. He had stopped shaking. There was even, at times, a glint of irony in his eyes . . .

. . . until the morning the prisoner heard footsteps in the next cell, and then loud screams.

They had come to fetch number 9, a son who had killed his father, to take him to the scaffold.

The next day, Heurtin, number 11, was in tears. But he said nothing. All he did was lie stretched out on his bunk with his teeth clenched and his face to the wall.

When Maigret got an idea into his head, it stayed anchored there for a long time.

He went to see Coméliau and told him: 'That man is either mad or he's innocent.'

'Impossible! In any case, sentence has been passed on him.'

Maigret, 1 metre 80 tall, powerful and as burly as a market porter, dug his heels in.

'Don't forget that the prosecution was unable to establish how he got back to Paris from Saint-Cloud. He didn't take the train. He didn't get on a tram. He didn't walk back!'

Jokes were made at his expense.

'Would you like to try an experiment?'

'You'll have to take this to the minister!'

And Maigret, solemn and stubborn, did so. He himself wrote the note which gave Heurtin the escape plan.

'Listen! Either there were others in it with him, and he'll think the note is from them, or there weren't, in which case he'll be on his guard and suspect a trap. I'll take full responsibility for him. You have my absolute word that he won't escape.'

The inspector's stolid, calm, rock-hard face was a sight to be seen!

The tussle lasted three days. He raised the spectre of a miscarriage of justice and the scandal which would follow sooner or later.

'But you're the one who arrested him!'

'Because, as a policeman, it's my job to draw logical conclusions from the material evidence presented.'

'And as a man?'

'I'm still waiting to be morally sure . . .'

'And?'

'Either he's mad or he's innocent.'

'Why doesn't he say anything?'

'The test I propose will tell us why.'

Then there were phone calls, discussions . . .

'You're putting your career on the line, detective chief inspector. Think about it!'

'I have thought about it.'

The note was duly passed to the prisoner, who had not shown it to anyone and, for the last few days, had eaten with a heartier appetite.

'So he wasn't surprised!' said Maigret. 'Therefore he was expecting something of the sort! Therefore he has accomplices who may have promised they'd get him out.'

'Unless he's pretending to be stupid! And then the minute he gets outside, he'll give you the slip. Have a care, detective chief inspector, your career . . .'

'But his head is at stake too . . .'

And now Maigret was ensconced in a leather chair in front of a window in a hotel bedroom. From time to time, he trained his binoculars on the Citanguette, where the dockers and boatmen went for a drink.

Down on the quayside, Inspector Janvier was kicking his heels, trying to look inconspicuous.

Dufour – as Maigret had observed for himself – had eaten grilled chitterlings and mashed potato and was now drinking a glass of calvados.

The window of the upstairs bedroom was still shut.

'Operator, put me through to the Citanguette.'

'The line is busy.'

'Too bad! Cut them off!'

A moment later:

'Is that you, Dufour?'

The inspector did not waste words:

'He's still sleeping!'

There was a knock on the door. It was Sergeant Lucas. The pipe-smoke was so thick that it made him cough.

3. The Torn Newspaper

'Anything new?'

After briefly shaking the inspector's hand, Lucas perched on the edge of the bed.

'There is something, but it's nothing special. In the end, the managing director of Le Sifflet handed over a letter he got at around ten this morning about the Santé story.'

'Let me have it!'

The sergeant handed him a crumpled sheet of paper. It was covered with marks in blue pencil, because at Le Sifflet they had simply cut a few passages from the note and linked the remaining sentences together before sending it for printing.

There were still typesetter's marks on it and the initials of the linotype operator who had set it up.

'A sheet of paper with the top cut off, probably to eliminate some printed matter or other,' said Maigret.

'Absolutely! That's what I thought straight away. And I also reckoned the letter was probably written in a café. I've seen Moers, who claims he can recognize the writing paper of most of the cafés in Paris.'

'Did he find anything?'

'Took him less than ten minutes. The paper comes from the Coupole on Boulevard Montparnasse. I've just come from there . . . Unfortunately, they get over a thousand customers through the doors every day, and more than fifty people ask for something to write on.'

'What did Moers make of the handwriting?'

'Nothing yet. I'm going to have to give the letter back to him, and he'll do the usual tests on it. Meanwhile, if you want me to go back the Coupole . . . ?'

Maigret had not taken his eyes off the Citanguette. The nearest factory had just opened its gates for a crowd of workers, most on bikes, who could be seen vanishing into the grey dusk.

On the ground floor of the bistro, a single electric light had been turned on, and the inspector could follow the comings and goings of the customers.

There were half a dozen of them standing at the counter, and one or two of them were eyeing Dufour suspiciously.

'What's he doing there?' asked Lucas when he picked out a fellow-officer in the distance. 'Oh, it's Janvier a bit further along, watching the water flow by.'

Maigret had stopped listening. From his vantage point he could see the foot of the spiral staircase which started behind the bar. A pair of legs had just appeared. They stopped briefly, then the figure of a man walked towards the others, and the pale head of Joseph Heurtin was lit by the full glare of the electric bulb.

With the same glance, the inspector picked out an evening paper which had just been put on a table.

'Lucas, do you know if some newspapers follow up news items in *Le Sifflet*?'

'I haven't seen a paper. But they must certainly recycle stories, if only to make life harder for us.'

The receiver was snatched off its cradle:

'Hello? The Citanguette . . . As quick as you can!'

For the first time since that morning, there was a sense of urgency about Maigret. On the other side of the Seine, the landlord was speaking to Heurtin, doubtless asking him what he wanted to drink.

Would not the first priority of a man who had escaped from the Santé prison be to look at the newspaper, which he had only to reach out to take?

In the bar, Dufour had got up and was in the phone booth.

'Hello?'

'Listen, Dufour! There's a newspaper on that table. On no account must he see it!'

'So what must I . . . ?'

'Quick, he's just sat down. The paper's there, right under his nose . . .'

Maigret was on his feet now, very tense. If Heurtin read the article, it would be the finish of the experiment which had been set up with so much difficulty.

Now he could see the convicted man, who had collapsed on to the bench seat that ran along the wall, sitting with his elbows on the table and holding his head in both hands.

The landlord set down a glass of spirits in front of him.

Dufour was making his way into the bar to get the paper.

Although Lucas was not aware of the details of the situation, he had guessed and was also leaning at the window. For a brief moment, their view was blocked by a passing tug which had lit its white, green and red lights and was frantically blowing its hooter.

'That's it!' growled Maigret as Inspector Dufour walked into the main room of the bar.

With a casual movement, Heurtin had unfolded the paper. Was the item about him on the front page? Would he see it straight away?

And would Dufour have the presence of mind to avert the danger?

It was typical of the officer that, before making his move, he felt the need to turn and look out over the Seine towards the window where his chief was watching.

He didn't seem to be the right man for the job, slender and neat and tidy in a bistro heaving with rough and ready dockers and factory workers.

But he went up to Heurtin, pointed to the newspaper and must have said something like:

'Excuse me, that's mine.'

Customers at the bar turned round. The fugitive, taken aback, looked up at the man who had spoken to him.

Dufour did not back down, tried to grab the paper and leaned forward. At Maigret's side, Lucas muttered:

'Ah! . . . Careful!'

And that did it! The stand-off did not last long. Heurtin had got slowly to his feet, like a man who does not yet know what he is going to do.

His left hand was still clutching the edge of the newspaper, which the police officer had not released.

Suddenly, with his free hand, he seized a soda-water

siphon from the next table, and the glass flask smashed into the officer's skull.

Janvier was less than fifty metres away, by the river's edge. But he heard nothing.

Dufour staggered and fell against the counter, breaking two glasses.

Three men leaped on Heurtin. Two others were supporting the officer by the arms.

There must have been a noise, because Janvier finally stopped contemplating the reflections in the water, turned his head towards the Citanguette, started walking and then, after a few steps, broke into a run.

'Quick! . . . Take a taxi! . . . I want you down there!' Maigret ordered Lucas.

The younger man didn't hurry. He knew he'd get there too late.

As would Janvier, though he was on the spot . . .

The fugitive was struggling, shouting something. Was he accusing Dufour of being from the police?

But regardless of this, he was momentarily left free to move and he made the most of his chance to smash the electric lightbulb with the siphon, which he was still clutching.

Maigret stood motionless, gripping the window safety rail with both hands. On the quayside below him, a taxi was just setting off. A match was struck in the Citanguette but went out immediately. Despite the distance, Maigret was ninety per cent certain that a shot had been fired.

Those minutes were interminable. The taxi, which had crossed the bridge, was limping along the unmade, rut-scarred road which ran along the opposite bank of the Seine.

It was moving so slowly that when it was still 200 metres from the Citanguette Sergeant Lucas jumped out and started running. Perhaps he had heard the shot being fired?

The shrill blast of a whistle. Lucas or Janvier was calling for assistance.

Then inside the bistro, behind the filthy windows with their raised letters spelling out *Consume your own food here* – with the *C* and the *f* missing – a candle was lit, which illuminated figures bending over a body.

But the view was unclear. The figures, so badly lit and seen from a distance, were unrecognizable.

Without moving from his window, Maigret was speaking into the telephone in a hushed voice:

'Hello? . . . Is that Grenelle police station? . . . I want men, now, in cars, in position around the Citanguette . . . And I want a man arrested if he tries to escape: tall, with a large head and pasty face . . . And send for a doctor . . .'

Lucas was now on site. His taxi had parked outside one of the front windows and was obstructing Maigret's view of part of the interior of the bistro.

Standing on a chair, the landlord was replacing the light-bulb, and once more the room was flooded with harsh light.

The phone rang.

'Hello? Is that you, detective chief inspector? . . . Coméliau here . . . I'm at home, yes . . . I have guests for dinner . . . But I needed to be reassured that . . .'

Maigret remained silent.

'Hello? Don't hang up . . . Are you still there?'

'I'm still here.'

'Well? . . . I can hardly hear you . . . Have you seen the evening papers? . . . They've all picked up on the revelations in *Le Sifflet* . . . I think it would be a good idea to . . .'

Janvier ran out of the Citanguette, sped off to the right into the shadow that shrouded the patch of waste ground.

'That apart, is everything going along well?'

'Everything's fine,' shouted Maigret and hung up.

He was bathed in sweat. His pipe had dropped to the floor and the still-burning tobacco was starting to singe the carpet.

'Hello, operator? Get me the Citanguette!'

'I've just put a call through to you.'

'And now I'm asking you to connect me to the Citanguette . . . Is that clear?'

Then he could tell by the movement in the bistro that the phone was ringing.

The landlord started forwards, but Lucas beat him to it.

'Hello? . . . That you, sir?'

'Yes,' said Maigret wearily. 'Got away, did he?'

'Of course he did!'

'And Dufour?'

'I don't think it's serious . . . A nick on the scalp . . . He didn't even pass out.'

'Reinforcements from Grenelle are on the way.'

'It won't help . . . You know what it's like around here . . . With all these building sites and heaps of debris, factory yards and the back streets of Issy-les-Moulineaux . . .'

'Was there any shooting?'

'Someone fired a shot, but I haven't been able to establish who it was . . . They're all a bit dazed, quiet as lambs . . . They don't seem to have any idea about what happened.'

A car came round the corner of the quayside, dropped two policemen and then, a hundred metres further along, two more.

Four more officers got out when the car stopped outside the bistro, and one of them walked round to the back of the building to cover the rear exit. The usual drill.

'What do I do now?' asked Lucas after a moment's silence.

'Nothing . . . Organize a search party, on the off-chance . . . I'm on my way.'

'Has a doctor been sent for?'

'Done.'

The girl who operated the switchboard also manned the hotel's reception desk. She gave a start when she saw a large shadow loom up before her.

Maigret was so calm, so cool, and his face was so hermetically closed, that he did not seem to be made of flesh and blood.

'How much?'

'Are you leaving?'

'How much?'

'I'll have to ask the manager . . . How many phone calls have you had? . . . Just a moment.'

But as she got to her feet, the inspector grabbed her by the arm, forced her to sit down again and placed a 100-franc note on the desk.

'That cover it?'

'I think so . . . Yes . . . But . . .'

He left with a sigh, walked slowly along the pavement and crossed the bridge without ever quickening his step.

At one point, he felt his pocket for his pipe, failed to locate it and probably took it as a sign that boded no good, for his lips curved into a bitter smile.

A handful of men from the barges had gathered outside the Citanguette but showed only a mild interest. The week before, two Arabs had killed each other on the same spot. The previous month, a sack containing the legs and torso of a woman had been fished out of the water with a boat-hook.

The rich apartment blocks of Auteuil were visible, obscuring the horizon on the other side of the Seine. The carriages of a Métro train rattled over a bridge nearby.

It was drizzling. Uniformed officers were tramping up and down, shining the pale discs of their electric torches all around them.

In the bar, Lucas was the only man standing. Customers who had seen or taken part in the scuffle were sitting in a line along the wall.

The sergeant moved from one to the other, checking their papers, while they eyed him resentfully.

Dufour had already been carried out to a police car, which drove off as smoothly as it could.

Maigret said nothing. With his hands in the pockets of his overcoat, he peered around him, slowly, and the look in his eyes was one of infinite gloom.

The landlord started to tell him something.

'Inspector, I swear that when . . .'

Maigret shut him up with a gesture then went up to an Arab, whom he examined from head to foot. The man's face turned grey.

'Are you working these days?'

'Yes. For Citroën . . . I . . .'

'How much longer before the court order banning you from showing your face around here is lifted?'

And Maigret nodded to a uniformed officer. It meant: 'Take him away!'

'Inspector!' cried the North African as he was being propelled towards the door. 'I can explain . . . I haven't done nothing!'

Maigret wasn't listening. The papers of a Pole were not quite in order.

'Take him away!'

And that was it! Dufour's revolver was found on the floor with one empty shell beside it. There were also the shattered remains of the siphon and the lightbulb. The newspaper had been torn, and there were two splashes of blood on it.

'What do you want to do with them?' asked Lucas, who had finished examining the men's papers.

'Let them go.'

Janvier did not reappear for another quarter of an hour. He found Maigret slumped in one corner of the bar with Sergeant Lucas. His shoes were spattered with mud, and there were dark stains on his raincoat.

He did not need to say anything. He sat down beside them.

Maigret, who looked as though he was thinking about something quite different, stared vaguely up at the counter, behind which the landlord stood, looking meek and contrite, and called:

'Rum!'

Again, his hand felt in his pockets for his pipe.

'Give me a cigarette,' he breathed to Janvier.

Janvier wished he could have thought of something to say. But he felt so devastated when he saw his chief's sagging shoulders that all he could do was sniff and turn his head away.

In his apartment overlooking the Champ-de-Mars, Coméliau the magistrate was hosting a dinner for twenty guests which was scheduled to be followed by an informal gathering where there would be dancing.

Meanwhile, Dufour had been laid on a steel table, and one of the Grenelle doctors got into a white gown while he watched his instruments being sterilized.

'Do you think the scar will be visible?' Dufour asked. The way he was lying meant that all he could see was the ceiling. 'The skull's not cracked, is it?'

'Of course not! It just needs a few stitches.'

'And will the hair grow back? . . . Are you sure? . . .'

The doctor, his forceps gleaming in his hand, nodded to his assistant to hold the patient still.

The patient choked back a cry of pain.

4. General Headquarters

Maigret did not flinch once, did not register the slightest trace of protest or impatience.

Solemn-faced, his features drawn, he listened to the end with deference and humility.

Perhaps his Adam's apple may have suddenly twitched at the moments when Monsieur Coméliau was at his most inflexible and vehement.

Thin, excitable and tense, the examining magistrate was pacing up and down in his office. He spoke so loudly that remand prisoners who were waiting in the corridor to be seen must have overheard snatches of what he was saying.

At times, he would pick up an object, which he briefly juggled in his hands before slamming it down again on his desk.

The clerk of the court was embarrassed and lowered his eyes, Maigret stood there and waited, a full head taller than the magistrate.

After a final reproving word, Coméliau scrutinized the face of the man before him but then looked away because, after all, Maigret was a man of forty-five who for twenty years had devoted himself to the most varied and delicate kinds of police business.

And above all, he was a man!

'But haven't you got anything to say for yourself?'

'I have just informed my superiors that they will have my resignation within ten days if I have failed to deliver the guilty man to them.'

'In other words, failed to get your hands on Joseph Heurtin.'

'To deliver the guilty man to them,' repeated Maigret simply.

The magistrate jumped like a jack-in-the-box.

'So you still think . . . ?'

Maigret remained silent. Monsieur Coméliau snapped his fingers and said hurriedly:

'I think we'll leave it there, if you don't mind. Go on like this and you'll drive me crazy . . . When you've got something, phone me.'

The inspector made his farewell and walked along the familiar corridors. But before going down to the street, he climbed up to the top floor, under the eaves of the Palais de Justice, and pushed open the door of the police forensic labs.

One of the specialists, seeing him suddenly standing in front of him, was struck by his appearance and, as he held out his hand, asked:

'Things not so good?'

'Everything's fine, thanks.'

He was staring, but at nothing in particular. He kept his dark overcoat on and his hands in its pockets. He looked like a man who, after a long journey, sees old, familiar places with new eyes.

It was with those eyes that he glanced through the photographs which had been taken the previous evening in a flat which had been burgled and read the record cards which one of his colleagues had sent for.

In one corner, a man, young, clean-shaven, tall and thin, with short-sighted eyes behind thick lenses, was watching him, looking surprised and apprehensive.

On his bench were magnifying glasses in all strengths, scraper-erasers, tweezers, bottles of ink, reagents plus a glass screen lit by a strong electric lamp.

The man was Moers, and he specialized in the study of paper, inks and handwriting.

He knew that it was him that Maigret had come to see.

Yet the inspector had not looked his way once, but instead had wandered around aimlessly.

Eventually, he took a pipe from his pocket, lit it and said in a voice that did not ring quite true:

'Right, then. Let's get to work!'

Moers, who knew where the inspector had just come from, got the message but pretended not to have noticed that something seemed wrong.

Maigret took his top coat off, yawned and exercised the muscles of his face, as if he were trying to become himself again. He grabbed the back of a chair, dragged it close to the young man, straddled it and said affectionately:

'So, Moers?'

It was over. He had finally shrugged off the weight he'd been carrying on his shoulders.

'So what have you got?'

'I spent all night on the note. It's a pity it has been fingered by so many people. There's no point looking for prints on it now . . .'

'I wasn't counting on anything.'

'I spent over an hour this morning at the Coupole . . . I tested all the inkwells. Do you know the place? There are several separate rooms: first, the main café area, part of which becomes a restaurant at meal times. Then there's the room on the first floor, the terrace outside and finally a small American-type saloon bar on the left, where all the regulars go.'

'I know it.'

'It was the ink in the saloon bar that was used to write the note. The words were written with the left hand, not by a left-handed person, but by someone who knows that almost everything that is written with the left hand has a family resemblance.'

The letter sent to *Le Sifflet* was still displayed on the glass screen in front of Moers.

'One thing is certain. Whoever sent it is an educated man, and I'd swear that he speaks and writes fluently several languages. Now, if I try my hand at graphology . . . But we're straying from the realm of the exact sciences.'

'Stray away.'

'Well, if I'm not very mistaken, we have here someone exceptional. Very obviously, intelligence way above average. But the most disturbing thing is a mixture of strong will and weakness, coldness and emotivity. It's a man's handwriting. Yet I have noted features denoting a definitely feminine nature . . .'

Moers was now riding his hobby horse. He grew pink with pleasure. Unconsciously Maigret gave a little smile, and the young man looked embarrassed:

'Of course, I know all this isn't very clear and that any examining magistrate wouldn't even listen to the end of what I have to say. Even so . . . Look, sir, I'd bet that the man who wrote this letter is suffering from serious illness and knows it . . . If he'd used his right hand, I could tell you a lot more. Oh! I forgot, there's one more thing. There were stains on the paper, though they might have been left there in the print-room. But one of these stains is of café au lait. And lastly, the top of the sheet was not cut off with a knife, but with a round object, like a spoon.'

'So, the note was written yesterday morning, in the bar of the Coupole, by a customer who'd ordered a café au lait and speaks several languages . . .'

Maigret stood up, held out his hand and murmured:

'Thanks for that. Now, if you'll let me have the note back . . .'

He left and growled a goodbye to the other people there. As the door closed behind him, someone said with a certain admiration:

'See that? For someone who's taken a tough blow . . . !'

But Moers, whose worship of Maigret was well known, glared at him. The man said no more and went back to the analysis he was engaged on.

Paris was wearing the cheerless face it always has in the unlovely days of October. Harsh daylight fell from a sky which resembled a dirty ceiling. Traces of the previous night's rain still glistened on the pavements.

The pedestrians had the grim air of people who have not yet adapted to winter.

During the night, orders of the day had been typed up at the Préfecture, taken by messenger to various police stations and sent by telegraph to all gendarmerie head-quarters, customs posts and the railway police.

As a result, while the crowds walked past, all police officers, as well as uniformed constables and inspectors in the Highways Department, the Vice Squad, the hotel and drugs agencies – had the same description clearly in their minds and stared at passers-by, hoping to find the man who fitted it.

It was like this from one end of Paris to the other. It was the same in the suburbs. Gendarmes patrolling the main roads demanded to see the papers of every tramp and vagrant.

On trains, at frontiers, people were surprised at being questioned more closely than usual.

The hunt was on for Joseph Heurtin, sentenced to death by the Seine Assizes, who had escaped from the Santé prison after a scuffle with Inspector Dufour in the bar of the Citanguette.

When he made his escape, all he had left was twenty-two francs in his pocket, said the service notes which Maigret had written.

The inspector left the Palais de Justice unaccompanied, without even calling in at his office on the Quai des Orfèvres, caught a bus to Bastille and rang the bell of a door on the third floor of a building in Rue du Chemin-Vert.

There was a smell of iodoform and boiled chicken. A woman who had not yet had time even to comb her hair said:

'Ah! He'll be ever so pleased to see you . . .'

Inspector Dufour was in bed in his room. He looked dejected and tense.

'How are you, son?'

'Mustn't grumble. They say my hair won't grow on scar tissue and that I'll have to wear a wig.'

Just as he had done in the lab, Maigret paced around the room like a man who doesn't know where to put himself. Eventually, he muttered:

'Do you blame me?'

Dufour's wife, who was still young and pretty, was standing in the frame of the door.

'Him? Blame you? Since first thing this morning he's been telling me over and over how worried he is about how you're going to get out of the fix you're in . . . He wanted me to go down to the post-office and ring you up!'

'Oh, no need to worry. Right then . . . I'll be seeing you,' said the inspector. 'I must be off.'

He did not go home, although he lived only 500 metres from there, in Boulevard Richard Lenoir. He began walking, because he needed to walk, needed to feel the indifferent crowd brush against him.

As he progressed through Paris in this frame of mind, the dejected air of earlier that morning, which made him look like a schoolboy who had been caught red-handed, began to fade. His features hardened. He smoked pipe after pipe, as he did on his good days.

Monsieur Coméliau would have been very surprised, and doubtless indignant, if he had suspected that the least of the inspector's worries was to find Joseph Heurtin.

That, for Maigret, was a secondary issue. The condemned man had to be somewhere in the middle of several million people. But he was convinced that the day he needed him, he'd easily be able to get hold of him.

No, he was thinking of the letter written at the Coupole. And also, and maybe more, of one question he reproved himself for having failed to ask during his first investigation.

But back in July everyone had been so convinced of Heurtin's guilt! The examining magistrate had taken over the inquiry himself from the start, thus sidelining the police.

'The crime was committed at Saint-Cloud at about two in the morning. Heurtin was back in Rue Monsieur-le-Prince before four. He didn't take a train or a tram or any other form of public transport. Nor did he take a taxi. His three-wheeled carrier never left his employer's premises in Rue de Sèvres.

'And he wouldn't have had time to come back on foot. If he had, he would have had to run all the way without stopping!'

The streets of Montparnasse were bustling with life. It was half past twelve. Though it was autumn, the terraces of the four large cafés which stood in a row just by Boulevard Raspail were heaving with customers, eighty per cent of whom were foreigners.

Maigret walked to the Coupole, found the entrance to the American Bar and went in.

There were just five tables, all taken. Most of the customers were perched on high bar stools or stood at the counter.

The inspector heard someone ordering:

'A Manhattan!'

And he added casually:

'Same here.'

He belonged to the generation that was raised on brasseries and beer. The bartender pushed a dish of olives under his nose, which he ignored.

'Do you mind if I . . . ?' asked a young Swedish girl with hair that was more yellow than blonde.

The place was crawling with people. A hatch in the rear wall was constantly opening and closing, and from the kitchen came a stream of olives, potato chips, sandwiches and hot drinks.

Four waiters shouted orders constantly amid a clatter of plates and the rattle of glasses, while customers called out to each other in a variety of languages.

And the overall impression was that customers, barmen, waiters and décor fused and formed a single, homogeneous identity.

The crowd intermingled as if they knew each other, and everybody – from the young woman, the big industrialist who had stepped out of his limousine with a group of high-spirited friends to the Estonian art student – called the head bartender Bob.

People talked to each other without being introduced, like old friends. A German spoke English with an American, and a Norwegian used a mix of three different languages as he tried to make himself understood by a Spaniard.

There were two women whom everyone knew, and one

of them Maigret recognized, though she was less slender now, older, but dressed in furs, as the young girl he'd once been ordered to escort to Saint-Lazare women's prison after the police had carried out a raid in Rue de la Roquette.

Her voice was hoarse, her eyes looked tired, and people shook her hand as they passed. She held court at her table, as if she embodied in her sole person the uneasy mix that surged around her.

'Do you have anything I can write with?' Maigret asked a barman.

'Not when we're serving aperitifs. You'll have to try in the brasserie.'

Among the noisy groups were a few customers who were alone. It was perhaps the most striking aspect of the place.

On the one hand, there were people who talked in loud voices, were never still, ordered round after round of drinks and drew attention to themselves in clothes which were as luxurious as they were eccentric.

On the other, there were individuals who seemed to have come from the four corners of the earth solely to be part of this brilliant company.

There was, for example, one young woman who could not have been more than twenty-two. She wore a slim-fitting black suit, well cut and comfortable, but it had obviously been pressed many times.

She cut an odd figure, weary and unsure of herself. She had put a sketch pad down beside her. And in the middle of all those people drinking aperitifs costing ten francs each, she sipped a glass of milk and nibbled a croissant.

This at one o'clock in the afternoon! It was obviously her lunch. She made the most of being there to read a Russian newspaper which the management made available for customers.

She neither heard nor saw anything. She ate her croissant slowly and from time to time drank a mouthful of milk, oblivious of the group sitting at her table, who were on to their fourth cocktail.

No less conspicuous was a man whose hair alone could not fail to attract attention. It was red, curly and exceptionally long.

He wore a dark suit which was shiny and tired, and a blue shirt with no tie. His collar was undone, and the shirt open on his chest.

He was ensconced at the far end of the bar, and the way he sat marked him out as a fixture, a regular whom no one would dare disturb. He was eating a pot of yogurt, spoonful by spoonful.

Were there even five francs in his pocket? Where had he come from? Where was he going? And how did he manage to get hold of the few coins he needed to pay for the yogurt, which was probably his only meal of the day?

Like the Russian girl, he had an eager gleam in his eyes and tired-looking eyelids, but there was also something infinitely disdainful and haughty in the cast of his features.

No one went out of their way to shake his hand or speak to him.

Suddenly, the revolving door admitted a man and woman, and in the mirror Maigret recognized the Crosbys, who had just got out of an American car worth at least 250,000 francs.

He could see it parked at the kerb. It was all the more eye-catching because the bodywork was entirely nickel-plated.

William Crosby held his hand over the mahogany counter between two customers who stood to one side, shook the bartender's fingers and said:

'How are you today, Bob?'

Meanwhile Mrs Crosby rushed over to the blonde Swedish girl, kissed her cheek and started speaking volubly in English.

None of them needed to order. Bob steered a whisky and soda in Crosby's direction, made a Jack Rose for the girl and asked:

'Back from Biarritz so soon?'

'We only stayed three days. It rains down there even more than it does here.'

Then Crosby caught sight of Maigret and nodded to him.

He was a tall man of about thirty, with brown hair, and he moved with loose-limbed grace.

Of all those assembled in the bar at that moment, he was the one whose elegant appearance was freest of bad taste.

He shook hands perfunctorily and asked friends:

'What'll you have?'

He was rich. At the door was a sports car, which he used for driving to Nice, Biarritz, Deauville or Berlin, as the fancy took him.

He had lived in a palace in Avenue Georges-V for a number of years and from his aunt had inherited, in addition to the villa at Saint-Cloud, fifteen or twenty million francs.

Mrs Crosby was petite but vivacious and she never stopped talking, mixing English and French with an inimitable accent all in a high-pitched voice which was enough for anyone to identify her without actually having to see her.

Maigret was separated from them by a number of customers. A member of parliament he knew walked in and shook the young American's hand warmly.

'Shall we have lunch together?'

'Not today. We've been invited out.'

'Tomorrow then?'

'Fine. Let's meet here.'

A messenger boy came in and called: 'Telephone for Monsieur Valachine!'

A man stood up and made for the phone booths.

'Two Jack Roses, two!'

The clatter of plates. Background noise which grew louder.

'Can you change some dollars for me?'

'Check the exchange rate in the paper.'

'Suzy not here?'

'She just left. I think she's having lunch at Maxim's.'

Maigret had a thought for the fugitive with the hydrocephalic head and long arms who was submerged in the madding crowd of Paris with just a little over twenty francs in his pocket and was even then being hunted high and low by the entire police force of France.

He remembered the pale face he had seen slowly climbing up the dark wall of the Santé.

Then Dufour's voice on the phone:

'*He's sleeping . . .*'

He'd slept for a whole day!

Where was he now? And why, yes, why on earth would he have killed this Mrs Henderson, whom he'd never met and from whom he had stolen nothing?

'Do you drop by here sometimes for an aperitif?'

The voice was William Crosby's. He had approached Maigret and was offering him his cigarette case.

'No thanks. I only smoke a pipe.'

'But you'll have something to drink? Whisky?'

'I've got a drink, as you see.'

Crosby looked slightly put out.

'Do you speak English, Russian and German?'

'Just French.'

'So the Coupole must sound like the tower of Babel to you! I've never seen you here before. By the way, is there any truth in what they're saying?'

'What do you mean?'

'You know . . . the murderer . . . ?'

'Oh there's no need to worry.'

Crosby let his eyes settle on him for a moment.

'Come on! Won't you give us the pleasure of your company and have a drink with us? My wife would be delighted. Allow me to introduce Mademoiselle Edna Reichberg, daughter of a paper manufacturer in Stockholm. She was skating champion last year at Chamonix. Edna, Detective Chief Inspector Maigret.'

The Russian girl in the black suit still had her nose deep in her newspaper, and the man with red hair was meditating, with his eyes shut, in front of the stone pot he'd scraped to get at the very last smudge of yogurt.

Through a forced smile, Edna said:

'So pleased to meet you.'

She gripped Maigret's hand firmly then returned, in English, to her conversation with Mrs Crosby while William said apologetically:

'Do you mind? I'm wanted on the phone. Two whiskies, Bob . . . You will excuse me, won't you? . . .'

Outside, the nickel-plated motor gleamed in the grey light and a pitiful figure shuffled round it, approached the Coupole, dragging one leg, and paused a moment outside the revolving door.

Red-rimmed eyes peered in while a waiter was already walking over to order this seedy tramp to move on.

The police, in Paris and elsewhere, were still hunting for the prisoner who had gone over the wall at the Santé prison.

And here he was, within hailing distance of the inspector!

5. The Man Who Liked Caviar

Maigret did not move. He did not even give a start. At his side, Mrs Crosby and the Swedish girl were chatting away in English, sipping cocktails. The inspector was so close to the latter, because the bar room was so small, that with every movement she made her supple body brushed against his.

Maigret managed somehow to grasp that they were talking about someone named José, who had flirted with her at the Ritz and offered her cocaine.

They were both laughing. William Crosby, rejoining them from the phone booth, apologized again to the inspector:

'You really must excuse me. It was about my car. I want to sell it and buy another one.'

He squirted a splash of soda water into their glasses.

'Cheers!'

Outside, it seemed that the curious silhouette of the convicted criminal was being literally blown around the terrace of the bar.

In getting away from the Citanguette, Joseph Heurtin had apparently lost his cap, with the result that he was now bare-headed. His hair had been cropped very short in prison so that his ears now stuck out even more than ever. His shoes no longer had either colour or shape.

And where had he slept that his suit should be so creased and covered with so much dust and mud?

If he had been holding his hand out to passers-by, that would have explained his presence there, for he looked like the most pitiful specimen of human flotsam. But he was not begging. And he wasn't selling shoe-laces or pencils.

He shambled up and down, tossed this way and that by the ebb and flow of the passing crowd, sometimes drifting away for a few metres then returning as though he were fighting against a strong current.

His cheeks were covered with brown stubble. He looked thinner.

But it was mainly the eyes which made him so unnerving, for he never took them off the bar and went on trying to see through the steamed-up windows.

Then he got as far as the entrance once more, and Maigret thought he was about to push the door open.

The inspector was smoking anxiously. His forehead was damp with sweat. His nerves were stretched so tight that he had the feeling that his senses had been heightened by a factor of ten.

It was a special moment. Only minutes before he had had the appearance of a man defeated, of being out of his depth. The case had slipped through his fingers, and there was nothing to reassure him that he could pick up the pieces.

He sipped his whisky slowly while Crosby, out of politeness, half turned towards him while participating in the conversation between his wife and Edna.

Strangely enough, without trying, without even being aware of doing so, Maigret was missing no part of this complex scene.

There were many people milling restlessly all round him. There was such a multiplicity of different sounds that they all blended into a single noise which was as indistinct as the surge of the sea. There were people talking, gesticulating, posing . . .

He saw it all: the man sitting in front of his yogurt pot, the tramp who kept being irresistibly drawn back to the door, Crosby's smile, the face which his wife made as she applied her lipstick, the energetic movements of the bartender as he made egg-nog in his cocktail shaker . . .

And customers leaving one after the other . . . The remarks they exchanged:

'Tonight? Here?'

'Try to bring Léa.'

Gradually the bar emptied. It was half past one. From the adjoining room came the sound of forks.

Crosby laid a 100-franc note on the counter.

'Are you staying?' he asked Maigret.

He had not yet noticed the man outside but he would come face to face with him when he left.

Maigret was waiting so impatiently for that moment it almost hurt.

Mrs Crosby and Edna said goodbye with nods and smiles.

It so happened that Joseph Heurtin was then less than two metres from the door. One of his shoes had lost its lace. It seemed likely that at any moment a policeman would ask to see his papers or tell him to move on.

The door swung on its hinges. Crosby, bare-headed, made for his car. The two women followed, laughing at something funny one of them had said.

And nothing at all happened! Heurtin did not look harder at the Americans than at the rest of the passers-by. And neither William nor his wife paid any attention to him.

All three got into the car. The door slammed shut.

People were still leaving, forcing back the escaped prisoner, who had come nearer once more.

All at once, in the mirror, Maigret caught sight of a face, two flashing eyes beneath thick eyebrows, and the faintest of smiles which pulsed with sarcasm.

Then the lids dropped over those all-too-eloquent eyes, though not quickly enough to prevent Maigret having the impression that it was at him that the sarcasm was directed.

The man who had been watching him, and who was now not watching anybody or anything in particular, was the man with red hair who had been eating yogurt.

When an Englishman who had been reading *The Times* had gone, there was no one left on the high bar stools, and Bob said:

'I'm going to lunch.'

His two assistants wiped the mahogany counter, cleared away the glasses and the half-eaten bowls of olives and potato chips.

But there were still two customers at the tables: the man with red hair and the Russian girl in black. Neither seemed aware that they were alone in the bar.

Outside, Joseph Heurtin was still prowling around, and his eyes were so weary, his face so pale, that one of the waiters who had been watching him through the window said to Maigret:

'There's another poor devil who's going to fall down in a fit at any moment . . . It's as if they just can't keep away from café terraces. I'll just go and get a porter . . .'

'Don't do that.'

Yogurt man was within hearing distance. Yet Maigret hardly lowered his voice as he said:

'Go and phone the Police Judiciaire. Say you're phoning for me. Tell them to send two men here . . . preferably Lucas and Janvier . . . Got that?'

'Is it about the tramp?'

'Never mind why.'

The bar was completely quiet now that the noisy aperitif hour was over.

The red-haired man had not moved or reacted. The girl in black turned a page of her newspaper.

The other bartender was looking curiously at Maigret. The minutes ticked by, flowing drop by drop as it were, second by second.

The man behind the bar was doing his reckoning up. There was a rustle of banknotes and a jingle of coins. The one who had gone to phone returned:

'They said they'd do it.'

'Thanks.'

The inspector's bulk dwarfed the slender bar stool. He smoked one pipe after another, unaware of emptying his glass of whisky, and forgot that he had had no lunch.

'Give me a café au lait.'

The words came from the corner where yogurt man was sitting. The waiter glanced at Maigret, gave a shrug and called towards the service hatch:

'Café au lait! Just the one!'

And, turning to the inspector, he murmured:

'That's all he'll order between now and seven o'clock . . . It's just the same with the other one there . . .'

He pointed his chin in the direction of the Russian girl.

Twenty minutes went by. Heurtin, wearying of walking up and down, had come to a stop on the edge of the pavement. A man getting into his car mistook him for a beggar and held out a coin, which he dared not refuse.

Did he have any of the twenty francs left? Had he eaten anything since the night before? Had he slept?

The bar still attracted him. Again he approached, sheepishly, keeping his eyes open for the waiters and porters who had already kicked him off the terrace.

But now it was a slack time, and he was able to stand outside the window, where he could be seen pressing his face to the glass, flattening his nose comically, while his small eyes peered inside.

The red-haired man was raising his cup of coffee to his lips. He did not turn to look outside.

So how was it that the same smile as before now made his eyes glint?

A Coupole employee, who could not have been more

than sixteen, shouted at the ragged man, who moved away yet again, dragging one foot.

Sergeant Lucas got out of a taxi, came in, obviously surprised, then looked all round the almost deserted bar with even greater astonishment.

'Was it you who . . . ?'

'What'll you have?'

And in a whisper:

'Take a look through the window.'

Lucas took a moment to locate the figure outside. His face lit up.

'Well I'll be damned! So you managed to . . .'

'I did nothing at all . . . Waiter! Cognac!'

The Russian girl called out in a strong accent:

'Waiter, bring me *Illustration*. Also business telephone directory.'

'Drink up, Lucas. I want you to go out and keep an eye on him, all right?'

'You don't think it would be better to . . . ?'

And one of the sergeant's hands could be seen feeling for his handcuffs.

'Not yet . . . Go to it.'

Maigret's nerves were so taut that, for all his outward calm, he almost crushed the glass in his large hand as he drank from it.

The man with red hair seemed in no hurry to leave. He wasn't reading, he wasn't writing, he was looking at nothing in particular. And, outside, Joseph Heurtin was still waiting!

At four in the afternoon, the situation had not changed in any way, except that the man on the run from the Santé had now moved to a bench, from which he kept his eyes trained on the entrance to the bar.

Maigret had eaten a sandwich, though he was not hungry. The Russian girl left after taking an age freshening her make-up.

So the only one now left in the bar was yogurt man. Heurtin had watched the girl leave without batting an eye. The lights were switched on, though the branched street lamps were not yet lit.

A drinks steward replenished the stock of bottles. Another employee quickly brushed the floor.

The sound of a spoon on a saucer, especially because it came from the corner where the man with red hair was sitting, came as much of a surprise to the bartender as to Maigret.

Without getting to his feet, without trying to conceal his disdain for such a niggardly customer, the bartender called out:

'One yoghurt, one café au lait. Three francs plus one franc fifty . . . that comes to four francs fifty!'

'Excuse me, I'd like you to bring me some caviar sandwiches.'

The voice was calm and collected. In the mirror, the inspector caught the laughter in the man's half-closed eyes.

The bartender raised the hatch.

'One caviar sandwich! Just the one!'

'Three!' said the customer, correcting him.

'Three caviar sandwiches! That's three!'

The bartender looked suspiciously across at the man and asked, in an ironic voice:

'You want vodka with that?'

'Yes, bring vodka.'

Maigret was trying hard to understand. The man had changed. His unusual stillness had vanished.

'And cigarettes!'

'Marylands?'

'Abdullahs.'

He smoked one while the sandwiches were being made and amused himself doodling on the packet. Then he ate so fast that he was on his feet by the time the bartender had barely returned to his post.

'Thirty francs for the sandwiches, six for the vodka, twenty-two for the Abdullahs plus the previous orders . . .'

'I'll call in and pay you tomorrow.'

Maigret frowned. He could still see Heurtin sitting on his bench.

'Just a moment . . . You'd best put that to the manager.'

The man with red hair gave a nod and, after returning to his seat, sat and waited. The manager appeared. He was in a dinner suit.

'What is it?'

'It's this gentleman. He wants to come back and pay tomorrow. Three caviar sandwiches, a packet of Abdullahs and so on.'

The customer did not seem at all embarrassed. He gave another polite nod, which seemed more mocking than ever, and confirmed what the bartender had said.

'Do you have any money with you?'

'Not a bean.'

'Do you live locally? I'll send a man with you . . .'

'There's no money at home either.'

'And yet you order caviar?'

The manager clapped his hands. A youth in uniform appeared.

'Go and fetch me a policeman.'

It was all happening quietly, with no fuss.

'Are you sure you have no money?'

'I told you.'

The youth, who had waited for this answer, left at a run. Maigret did not stir. Meanwhile, the manager stood there, calmly watching the passing interest in Rue Montparnasse.

From time to time, the bartender winked knowingly at Maigret as he wiped his bottles.

Three minutes had hardly passed when the youth came back with two officers on bicycles, which they parked outside.

One of them recognized the inspector and would have gone up to him if Maigret had not put him off with a frown. Meanwhile the manager explained simply and without unnecessary fuss:

'This gentleman ordered caviar, expensive cigarettes and so forth and now refuses to pay.'

'I have no money,' repeated the man.

At a nod from Maigret, the policeman simply said:

'Very well! You can come down to the station and explain yourself there. Follow me.'

'Can I offer you gentlemen a little something?' asked the manager.

'No, but thanks all the same.'

Trams, cars and crowds of people filled the boulevard over which the fading light was spreading thick fog. Before leaving, the man being led away lit another cigarette and gave a friendly wave to the bartender.

And as he passed Maigret, his eyes settled on him for just a few seconds.

'Hey! Get a move on! . . . And we don't want any trouble, all right?'

Then all three were gone. The manager went up to the counter.

'That wasn't the Czech we had to throw out last week, was it?'

'That's him,' said the bartender. 'He's here every day from eight in the morning until eight at night. And you're lucky if he orders a couple of coffees all day.'

Maigret had walked to the door. He was thus able to see Joseph Heurtin get up from his bench and stand stock still with his eyes on the two officers who were leading away the man who liked caviar.

But it was already too dark for Maigret to make out his features.

The three men had not gone a hundred metres before the tramp went off in the other direction, followed at a distance by Sergeant Lucas.

'Police Judiciaire!' the inspector said going back into the bar. 'Who is he?'

'I think he's called Radek . . . He has his letters sent here

'. . . You've seen all the letters we put up in the window. A Czech.'

'What does he do?'

'Nothing. He spends every day here in the bar . . . He thinks . . . He writes . . .'

'Do you know where he lives?'

'No.'

'Does he have any friends?'

'I don't think I ever remember seeing him speak to anybody.'

Maigret paid his bill, walked out, jumped into a taxi and barked:

'Take me to the local police station.'

When he got there, Radek was sitting on a bench, waiting until the station's senior inspector was ready to see him.

There were four or five foreigners who had come to register their addresses.

Maigret walked straight into the inspector's office, where a young woman was reporting a theft of jewels in a mixture of three or four central European languages.

'Are you here on a case?' said the inspector, rather taken aback.

'Please finish dealing with this lady.'

'I can't make out a word she's saying . . . She's been explaining the same thing over and over for the last half-hour.'

Maigret did not even smile, but the lady became angry, repeated her story point by point and held up her ringless fingers.

Finally, when she had gone, he said:

'You're about to see a man named Radek, or something along those lines. I'll be here. Fix it so that he has to spend a night in the cells, after which you let him go.'

'What's he done?'

'He ordered caviar and wouldn't pay.'

'At the Dôme?'

'No, the Coupole.'

A bell rang.

'Let's have Radek in.'

Radek, hands in pockets, strode into the office without a care in the world, settled down opposite the two men and waited, looking them straight in the eye, while a delighted smile played around his lips.

'You are charged with buying goods without money.'

The man nodded and began lighting a cigarette, which the inspector angrily snatched from his fingers.

'What have you got to say for yourself?'

'Not a thing.'

'You have a room somewhere? Enough money to live on?'

From his pocket, the man produced a filthy passport, which he placed on the desk.

'You realize you face two weeks in jail?'

'The sentence will be suspended,' said Radek, without turning a hair. 'I think you'll find that I have never been convicted of any offence.'

'It says here that you are a medical student. Is that correct?'

'Professor Grollet, who you must know by name, will tell you that I was his best pupil.'

And, turning to Maigret, with a hint of mockery in his voice:

'I assume that this gentleman also works for the police?'

6. The Inn at Nandy

Madame Maigret sighed but said nothing when, at seven next day, her husband left her after drinking his coffee without even noticing that it was scalding hot.

He had got home at one in the morning in uncommunicative mood. He went out again in a dogged frame of mind.

As he trudged through the corridors of the Préfecture, he was very aware in the colleagues he met, not just the inspectors but the office clerks too, of a sense of curiosity, even admiration tinged, perhaps, with a hint of commiseration.

But he shook their hands as perfunctorily as he had kissed his wife on the forehead, and the moment he was in his office he began poking the stove before stretching his overcoat, which was heavy from the rain, across a couple of chairs.

Then unhurriedly, and drawing gently on his pipe, he spoke into the phone: 'Get me Montparnasse police station.'

Mechanically he tidied the papers littering his desk.

'Hello? . . . Who is that? Ah, the duty sergeant. This is Detective Chief Inspector Maigret of the Police Judiciaire. Have you let Radek go? . . . Say again? . . . An hour ago? . . . Did you make sure that Inspector Janvier was there to

tail him? . . . Hello . . . speaking . . . He didn't sleep a
wink? He smoked all his cigarettes? . . . Thanks . . . No!
There's no point . . . If I need more information, I'll come
round . . .'

From his pocket he took the Czech's passport, which he
had kept: a small, greyish document embossed with the
national emblem of Czechoslovakia. Almost every page
was covered with stamps and visas.

According to the visas, Jean Radek, aged twenty-five,
born at Brno, father unknown, had resided in Berlin,
Mainz, Bonn, Turin and Hamburg.

His papers described him as a medical student. His
mother, Élisabeth Radek, had died two years earlier. Her
profession was given as 'servant'.

'What do you live on?' Maigret had asked the previous
evening in the office of the inspector in charge of Montparnasse police station.

The prisoner had replied with that jarring smile:

'Can I ask impertinent questions too?'

'Just answer the question.'

'When my mother was alive she used to send enough
for me to carry on with my studies.'

'What, out of a servant's wages?'

'Yes. I'm an only child. There's nothing she wouldn't
have done for me. Does that surprise you?'

'She's been dead for two years . . . Since then?'

'Some distant relatives have been sending me small
sums from time to time. And there are compatriots living
in Paris who help out as and when . . . And sometimes I
am asked to do translation work.'

'And file copy for *Le Sifflet*?'

'I don't understand.'

He had said this with an explicit irony which could be interpreted as: 'Keep going! You haven't pinned me down yet!'

Maigret had chosen to leave it there. There was no sign of Joseph Heurtin anywhere around the Coupole, nor of Sergeant Lucas. They had both vanished once more into Paris, one in the footsteps of the other.

'Hôtel Georges V,' Maigret had barked to the taxi-driver.

He had walked in just as William Crosby, wearing a dinner jacket, was changing a 100-dollar banknote at the hotel's foreign exchange desk.

'Are you looking for me?' he had asked when he noticed the inspector.

'No . . . unless you happen to know a man named Radek?'

People were walking in, through and out of the Louis XIV lobby. The clerk had counted out 100-franc notes, which were pinned together in bundles of ten.

'Radek . . . ?'

Maigret was looking directly into the eyes of the American, who did not flinch.

'No . . . but you could ask Mrs Crosby. She'll be down any moment now. We're dining in town with friends. It's a benefit gala at the Ritz.'

And on cue Mrs Crosby had emerged from the lift, cosily wrapped in a hooded ermine cape, and stared at the policeman with considerable surprise.

'What is it?'

'There's no need to be concerned. I'm looking for a man named Radek.'

'Radek? Is he staying here?'

Crosby had stuffed the notes into his pocket and held out his hand to Maigret.

'You must excuse me, we're running rather late.'

The car waiting outside glided smoothly forwards over the asphalt.

The phone rang loudly.

'Hello? Examining Magistrate Coméliau asking to speak to Detective Chief Inspector Maigret.'

'Say I'm not in yet.'

At this time of day, Coméliau must be phoning from home. No doubt he was in his dressing gown, busily eating his breakfast as he skimmed through the newspapers, lips quivering as usual with that nervous tremor of his.

'Listen, Jean. Has anyone else been asking for me? . . . Anyway, what did Coméliau want?'

'He wants you to call him the moment you get in. He'll be at home until nine, then after that he'll be in the prosecutor's office . . . Hello? . . . Wait! . . . A call for you . . . Hello? Hello? . . . Detective Chief Inspector Maigret? . . . I'll put Inspector Janvier through to you . . .'

A moment later, the call came through.

'That you, sir?'

'Disappear, did he?'

'Vanished, yes. I don't get it. I wasn't twenty metres behind him . . .'

'And . . . ? Out with it!'

'I'm still wondering how it could have happened. Especially since I'm certain he hadn't spotted me.'

'Carry on.'

'First he just ambled round the streets of Montparnasse. Then he walked into the station. It was the time of day when the suburban trains were arriving, and I closed up on him because I was afraid of losing him in the crowd.'

'But he went missing all the same!'

'Yes, but not in the crowd. He got into a train that had just arrived. He didn't buy a ticket. In the time it took me to ask a porter where the train was going while I kept one eye on his carriage, he had disappeared from his compartment. He must have got out of the other side of the train . . .'

'Good grief!'

'What do you want me to do now?'

'Go back to the Coupole and wait for me there . . . Don't be surprised by anything . . . And above all, stay calm!'

'I swear, sir . . .'

From the other end of the line, the voice of Inspector Janvier, who was only twenty-five, sounded like that of a small boy who was about to burst into tears.

'Right, then. I'll see you shortly.'

Maigret put the receiver down and then picked it up again.

'Hôtel Georges V? . . . Hello? . . . Yes . . . Has Monsieur William Crosby returned? . . . No . . . No need to bother him . . . What time did he get in? . . . Three o'clock? . . . And Madame Crosby was with him? . . . Thank you . . . Yes? . . . What's that? . . . He left instructions that he was not to be disturbed before eleven? . . . Thanks . . . No, there's no message . . . I'll see him myself.'

The inspector took a few moments to fill his pipe and even to check that there was enough coal on the fire.

At that moment, to anyone who did not know him closely, he would have given the impression of a man oozing confidence, striding unhesitatingly towards a certain goal. He thrust out his chest and blew the smoke from his pipe at the ceiling. When the office clerk brought him the morning newspapers, he was in a joky, cheerful mood.

But suddenly, the minute he was alone, he grabbed the telephone receiver:

'Hello? Has Lucas been asking for me?'

'Nothing yet, sir.'

Maigret's teeth bit hard in the stem of his pipe. It was 9 a.m. Joseph Heurtin had been missing since five in the afternoon of the previous day, having disappeared from Boulevard Raspail with Sergeant Lucas on his tail.

Was it likely that Lucas had been unable to find some way of phoning or of writing a note to give a passing uniformed officer?

Maigret expressed what he had at the back of his mind by asking the switchboard to connect him with Inspector Dufour. Dufour himself answered.

'Feeling better?'

'I'm already walking around the apartment. Tomorrow I hope to come into the office . . . But just wait until you see the scar it'll leave! . . . The doc took the bandage off last night, and I managed to get a glimpse of it . . . It makes you wonder how I didn't have my skull sliced open . . . But I assume that you've found the man at least?'

'Don't worry about that . . . Listen, I'm going to hang up now because I can hear someone ringing the switchboard and I'm expecting a call . . .'

It was stifling in the office. The stove was glowing white hot.

Maigret had been right. The moment he replaced the receiver, his phone rang. He heard Lucas' voice.

'Hello! Is that you, chief? . . . Don't cut me off, operator . . . Police business . . . Hello? Are you there?'

'I'm listening . . . Where are you?'

'Morsang.'

'Where?'

'It's a small village thirty-five kilometres from Paris, on the Seine.'

'And . . . where is *he*?'

'He's safe . . . He's in his own house!'

'Is Morsang anywhere near Nandy?'

'It's four kilometres away . . . I've come here so as not to give the game away . . . What a night I've had, sir.'

'Tell me about it.'

'At first, I thought he'd go on wandering around Paris for ever . . . He didn't look as if he knew where he was going . . . At eight o'clock, we both stopped at the soup kitchen in Rue Réaumur, and he waited around almost two hours for his grub . . .'

'Which means he has no money.'

'Then he set off again . . . It's amazing how drawn to the Seine he seems to be . . . He walked along it one way and then came back the other . . . Hello? . . . Don't cut us off! . . . Are you still there?'

'Go on.'

'In the end, he headed off towards Charenton along the riverbank . . . I was expecting him to doss down under a bridge . . . I really did! He was nearly out on his feet . . . But no! He passed Charenton and went on to Alfortville, where he didn't hesitate but set off on the road to Villeneuve-Saint-George . . . The road was sodden . . . Cars speeding past every thirty seconds . . . If I had to do that again . . .'

'You'd do it all over again! . . . Carry on.'

'That's how it was. Thirty-five kilometres of it! Can you imagine? It started to rain, and it came down harder and harder. He didn't seem to notice. At Corbeil I almost flagged down a taxi so it would be easier to keep tabs on him . . . But at six this morning, we were still walking, still one behind the other, through the woods which run from Morsang to Nandy.'

'How did he get into his house? Through the door?'

'Do you know the inn there? It's not up to much. A stopping-place for carters, a mixture of inn and café where you can get newspapers and cigarettes. I think it also serves as a general shop. But he went round it along an alleyway a metre wide and from there he climbed over a wall. Then I realized he'd gone into a small outhouse where they probably keep animals.'

'Is that everything?'

'More or less. Half an hour later, old man Heurtin came out to pin back the shutters and open the shop. He seemed pretty unconcerned. I went in for a drink, and he didn't seem upset in any way. On the way there, I'd been lucky enough to come across a gendarme on a bike. I asked him to let one tyre down and use that as an excuse to wait inside for me to come back.'

'Good!'

'Is that what you think? It's obvious you weren't the one who got covered in mud. My shoes are all mushy, like poultices. My shirt must be wet through. So what do I do now?'

'It goes without saying that you weren't carrying a case with a quick change of clothes?'

'If I'd had to carry a case as well! . . .'

'Go back there. Say anything, say you're waiting for a friend you've arranged to meet there.'

'Will you be coming?'

'No idea. But if Heurtin gets away yet again, it's very likely I'll explode.'

Maigret hung up and looked idly around him. He called to the office clerk through the half-open door:

'Listen, Jean. When I've gone, I want you to phone Monsieur Coméliau and tell him . . . er . . . tell him that everything is going well, and that I'll keep him informed . . . Got that? . . . And be nice . . . Use all the polite words you can think of.'

At eleven o'clock he was getting out of a taxi at the Coupole. The first person he saw as he pushed the door open was Inspector Janvier, who, like all rookies, thought he could convey a casual air by hiding three-quarters of his person behind an open newspaper without ever turning the pages.

In the corner opposite sat Jean Radek who was absently stirring his coffee with a spoon.

He was clean shaven and wearing a clean shirt. It was just possible that his curly hair had had a comb passed through it.

But the main impression he gave was one of intense inner jubilation.

The bartender had recognized Maigret and was readying himself to tip him off.

Behind his newspaper Janvier was also miming madly.

But Radek made their efforts unnecessary by calling out to Maigret directly:

'Would you like a drink?'

He had half risen from his seat. He was barely smiling, but there was no part of his face that did not proclaim the presence of a sharply intelligent mind.

Maigret walked over to him, thick-set and ponderous, grabbed the back of a chair with a hand capable of pulverizing it and sat down heavily.

'Back already?' he said, but his eyes were elsewhere.

'Your colleagues were very helpful. It seems I won't have to appear before a justice of the peace for a fortnight, because the courts are so overloaded . . . Look, it's too late now for coffee. What would you say to a glass of vodka and caviar sandwiches? Bartender!'

The bartender flushed until even his ears were red. He was visibly unsure about serving this very strange customer.

'I do hope that you're not going to make me pay in advance again. As you see, I'm with someone,' Radek went on.

And to Maigret he explained:

'These people just do not understand . . . Imagine, when I got here, he refused to serve me. He didn't say anything but went and fetched the manager. The manager asked me to leave. I was forced to lay down money on the table. Don't you find that amusing?'

He spoke the words solemnly, in a faraway voice.

'You will note that if I were some common swindler type, like one of those gigolos you probably spotted here yesterday, I'd be given any amount of credit. But I'm not just anybody! So you get my drift, inspector? We'll have to thrash it out one of these days, just the two of us. You probably won't understand it all. Still, you already think of yourself as one of the clever people.'

The bartender put the caviar sandwiches down on the table and said, not without a wink in Maigret's direction:

'Sixty francs.'

Radek smiled. In his corner, Inspector Janvier was still crouching behind his newspaper.

'A packet of Abdullahs,' ordered the red-haired Czech.

And while the cigarettes were being brought, he ostentatiously took from an outside pocket of his jacket a shabby 1,000-franc note, which he tossed on to the table.

'Now what were we saying, inspector? . . . Would you excuse me a moment? I've just remembered I must call my tailor.'

The phone booth was located at the far end of the brasserie, from which there were several exits.

Maigret did not move from where he was. But Janvier, needing no urging, followed their man at a distance.

And then they both came back, one behind the other, as they had left. With a look, Janvier confirmed that the Czech had indeed phoned his tailor.

7. Little Man

'Would you like a valuable piece of advice, inspector?'

Radek had lowered his voice as he leaned towards his companion.

'Actually I know what you'll think before you think it! But that is a matter of complete indifference to me. Here's my opinion anyway, my advice, if you prefer. Let it go! You are about to stir up a terrible hornets' nest.'

Maigret remained stock still, looking straight ahead of him.

'And you'll go on losing your way because you haven't a clue about any of it.'

Slowly the Czech was becoming excited, but in a muted way, so typical of the man. Maigret now noticed the man's hands, which were long, surprisingly white and dotted with freckles. They seemed to reach out and in their way be part, so to speak, of the conversation.

'Let's be clear that it's not your professionalism which I question. If you understand nothing, and I mean zero, it's because from the very start you've been working with facts which had been falsified. And once that is conceded, everything that has flowed from them is false too, no? And everything you will discover will also be false, and so on all down the line.

'On the other hand, the few points which might have given you something solid to work from you missed . . .

'Just one example. Admit that you have not noticed the role played by the Seine in this case. The villa at Saint-Cloud overlooks the Seine. Rue Monsieur-le-Prince is 500 metres from the Seine. The Citanguette, where the papers say the condemned man hid out after his escape, is by the Seine. Heurtin was born at Melun, on the Seine. His parents live at Nandy, which is on the banks of the Seine . . .'

The Czech's eyes were all laughter in a face which remained deadly serious.

'That must make you feel pretty foolish, no? It looks as if I'm throwing myself into your net, no? You don't ask me anything, yet here I am talking about a crime which you'd love to charge me with . . . But how? Why? I have no links with Heurtin, no links with Crosby, no links with Madame Henderson or her maid! All you have on me is that yesterday Joseph Heurtin came prowling round here and appeared to be staring at me.

'Maybe he was, maybe he wasn't. But that doesn't alter the fact that I walked out of this place escorted by two policemen.

'But what does that all prove?

'I tell you: you don't understand any of it and never will.

'And what am I doing in the midst of it all? Nothing! Or maybe everything!

'Now suppose that there is an intelligent man, a very intelligent man, who has no call on his time and spends every day thinking, who is unexpectedly presented with an opportunity to study a problem with a direct bearing on his special subject. Because criminality and medicine overlap . . .'

The unresponsiveness of Maigret, who did not even seem to be listening, was beginning to irk him. He raised his voice:

'Eh? So what do you say to that, inspector? Have you started admitting to yourself that you are all at sea? No? Not yet? Well allow me to point out that you were wrong, when you had a guilty man under lock and key, to let him go. Because not only might you be unable to find another suspect to put in his place, he might also slip through your fingers . . .

'Just now I mentioned unreliable facts. Shall I give you a new piece of incriminating evidence? And at the same time would you also like me to provide you with the excuse you need to arrest me?'

He drank his vodka down in one, leaned well back against the wall-bench and thrust one hand in an outside pocket of his jacket.

When he withdrew it, it was full of 100-franc notes in bundles of ten each fastened with a pin. There were ten bundles.

'You will observe that the notes are brand new. In other words, notes whose origin is easily traceable . . . Why not try? Go on, have fun! Unless you'd rather go home to bed, a course of action which I strongly advise.'

He stood up. Maigret remained seated and looked hard at Radek from head to foot as he produced a thick cloud of smoke from his pipe.

Customers began arriving.

'Are you going to arrest me?'

The inspector did not hurry to reply. He picked up the notes and examined them carefully before putting them in his pocket.

Eventually he too got to his feet, but so slowly that the Czech's face began to twitch. Maigret put one hand lightly on his shoulder.

It was Maigret in his prime, a Maigret who was sure of himself, imperturbable.

'Listen, little man . . .'

The words were in stark contrast with Radek's tone and with the nervy figure he cut and the tetchy look in his eyes, which shone with intelligence of an entirely different order.

Maigret was twenty years older than him, and it was obvious.

'*Listen, little man . . .*'

Janvier, who had overheard, tried hard not to laugh and also to contain his delight in rediscovering the chief he knew.

Maigret merely added, in the same off-hand good humour:

'We'll meet again one of these days, you'll see.'

Whereupon he nodded to the bartender, thrust both hands into his pockets and left.

'I think that they're the ones, but I'll go and check,' said the clerk in the Georges V as he inspected the banknotes which Maigret had just handed to him.

A moment later he was talking down the phone to the bank.

'Hello? Would you have the serial numbers of the hundred 100-franc notes which I sent a messenger round to collect yesterday morning?'

He wrote them down with a pencil, hung up and turned to the inspector.

'It's them, all right. I hope there's no problem, is there?'

'Not at all . . . Are Monsieur and Madame Crosby in their suite?'

'They went out half an hour ago.'

'Did you see them leave personally?'

'As clearly as I see you now.'

'The hotel has several exits, does it?'

'Two. But the second one is the service entrance.'

'You told me that Monsieur and Madame Crosby got back last night at around three. Have they had any visitors since then?'

They questioned the porter, the maid and the doorman.

In this way, Maigret had proof that the Crosbys had not left their suite between the hours of three and eleven o'clock in the morning, and that no one had had access to their rooms.

'And they did not send any letters via the messenger-boy either?'

A blank.

But there was also the fact that from four the previous afternoon until seven o'clock next morning, Jean Radek had been locked in the cells at Montparnasse police station, from which he could not have communicated with the outside.

But at seven that morning he had found himself in the street without a penny to his name. At around eight, he had shaken Janvier off his tail at Montparnasse station.

By ten, he had turned up at the Coupole, carrying a sum of at least 11,000 francs, 10,000 of which had certainly been in the pocket of William Crosby the previous evening.

'Mind if I have a look round upstairs?'

The manager hesitated at first, but in the end gave his authorization, and a lift whisked Maigret up to the third floor.

It was the standard luxury suite: two bedrooms, two bathrooms, sitting room and a dressing room.

The bed had not yet been made, and the breakfast things had not been cleared away. William Crosby's valet was brushing the American's dinner-jacket. In the next room an evening gown had been thrown over a chair.

Various objects had been left lying around: cigarette cases, a woman's handbag, a walking stick, a novel with the pages still uncut.

Maigret went back down and out on to the street, where he found a taxi to take him to the Ritz. There, the head-waiter confirmed that the Crosbys, accompanied by Miss Edna Reichberg, had been sitting at table 18 the night before. They had arrived around nine o'clock and had not left until two-thirty. The head-waiter had noticed nothing unusual.

'And the banknotes?' grunted Maigret to himself as he crossed Place Vendôme.

Suddenly he stopped and almost got caught by the mud-guard of a passing limousine.

'Why the devil did Radek show them to me? But that's not all: I'm the one who's got them now and I'd be hard put to come up with a legal explanation why . . . And then this connection with the Seine . . .'

Suddenly, without stopping to think twice about it, he hailed a cab.

'How long would you take to get to Nandy? It's a little further out than Corbeil.'

'An hour. The roads are slippery.'

'Let's go! But first stop at a tobacconist's.'

And Maigret, settling back comfortably into the car seat while the windows steamed up inside and gathered rain-drops outside, spent an hour in the way he liked best.

He smoked constantly, snug and warm in the great black overcoat which was famous on Quai des Orfèvres.

The outskirts slipped past, and then the October countryside, which allowed an occasional glimpse of the grey-green ribbon of the Seine between leafless trees.

'Radek could have had only one reason for talking and showing me the banknotes: he wanted to throw the inves-tigation momentarily off track by entangling me in a new mystery.

'But why? To give Heurtin time to get away? To com-promise Crosby?

'But in doing so he compromised himself!'

The words of the Czech came back to him:

'. . . from the very start you've been working with facts which had been falsified.'

By God! Wasn't it because he'd realized that Maigret had been given extra time to investigate even though the Assize court had delivered its verdict?

But how many facts had been 'falsified' and how had it been done? There was material evidence which could not possibly have been tampered with!

At a pinch, whoever murdered Mrs Henderson and her maid could have borrowed Heurtin's shoes in order to leave the marks of his soles in the villa.

The same could not be said about the fingerprints. Some had been found on items which had not moved from the crime scene during the night, such as curtains and bed linen!

So what facts had been falsified? Heurtin had unquestionably been seen at midnight in the Pavillon Bleu. And he had unquestionably got home in Rue Monsieur-le-Prince at four in the morning.

'You understand nothing and you will understand less and less!' announced Radek, who had surfaced at the heart of the case, while for months no one had even known he existed.

The day before, at the Coupole, William Crosby had not given the Czech a second glance.

And when Maigret had mentioned him by name, he had shown no reaction.

And that despite the fact that the bundles of 100-franc notes had moved from the pocket of one of them into the pocket of the other!

And Radek had made a point of telling the police about it! But there was more. It now seemed that Radek was pushing himself centre stage and casting himself for the leading role!

'He was free for exactly four hours between the moment he left the police station and the time I found him at the Coupole. During those four hours, he shaved and changed his shirt. And it was at some point during those few hours that the banknotes came into his possession.'

Maigret, who needed to feel some sort of certainty, found it by concluding:

'At the very least, that must have him taken half an hour! Therefore he didn't have enough time to go to Nandy.'

The village stands on the plateau which overlooks the Seine. Up on top, the west wind was blowing in gusts, bending the trees, while the brown ploughed fields, in which a solitary hunter looked no bigger than a full-stop, stretched away clear to the horizon.

'Where do you want me to drop you?' asked the driver, sliding back the glass panel between them.

'On the edge of the village . . . You can wait for me.'

There was only one long street and, halfway along it, a sign which said: 'Évariste Heurtin, proprietor'.

When Maigret pushed the door, a bell rang, but there was no one in the bar. The walls were decorated with colour-prints. But Sergeant Lucas' hat was hanging on a nail. Maigret called:

'Hello? Anyone about?'

He heard footsteps above his head, but at least five minutes went by before anyone decided to come down the stairs, which he could see at the end of a corridor.

Maigret saw a man of sixty or so, well built, with eyes that were unexpectedly fixed and staring.

'What do you want?' he asked from the corridor.

But he followed this up almost immediately with:

'Are you from the police too?'

The voice was neutral, the syllables indistinct and the innkeeper made no effort to say more. With a wave of his hand he motioned to the stairs, at whose foot he had remained standing, and then started slowly climbing up them.

Muffled sounds came from above. The stairs were narrow, and the walls whitewashed. When a door opened, the first thing Maigret saw was Sergeant Lucas by the window. His head was bowed and at first he did not notice him come in.

Then Maigret made out a bed with a figure leaning over it, and an old woman prostrate in a high-backed elbow chair.

The room was big, with exposed ceiling beams, very worm-eaten, and areas of peeling wallpaper. The pine floorboards creaked underfoot.

'Shut the door!' snapped the man who was leaning over the bed.

It was the doctor. His bag stood open on a round mahogany table. Lucas, looking haggard, approached Maigret.

'Here already? How did you manage it? It's less than an hour since I phoned.'

Bare-chested, his skin bluish-white, ribs showing through, the figure lying on the bed like a broken doll was Joseph Heurtin.

The old woman never stopped moaning. The eyes of the father, who was standing by the head of the fugitive's bed, were so vacant they were frightening.

'This way,' said Lucas. 'I'll bring you up to date.'

They left the room. On the landing outside, the sergeant hesitated a moment, then opened the door of another room, which had not yet been made up. Women's clothes were scattered everywhere. The window overlooked a yard where hens paddled around a sodden dung-heap.

'Well?'

'I've had a lousy morning, I can tell you! After ringing you I came straight back here and gave the gendarme the nod that he could go. What happened next I've worked out bit by bit . . .

'Old man Heurtin was in the bar with me. He asked if I wanted anything to eat. I was aware that he was eyeing me suspiciously especially when I said perhaps I'd be staying the night because I was waiting for someone.

'At one point, I heard whispering in the kitchen, which is at the end of the corridor, and I saw the landlord cock his ears in surprise.

'"Is that you, Victorine?" he called.

'It all went quiet for two or three minutes. Then the old woman came in with a very peculiar look on her face.

'It was the look of someone who has had a terrible shock and doesn't want to show it.

'"I'm going to fetch the milk," she said.

'"But it's not time . . . "

'She went all the same, clogs on her feet, a shawl over

her head, while her husband went off to the kitchen, where his daughter was by herself.

'I heard raised voices, sobs and one complete sentence which I could make out:

'"I should have known ... Just by the look on your mother's face ..."

'And out he went into the yard, at a run. He opened a door, obviously the door of the outhouse where Joseph Heurtin had hidden.

'He came back an hour later, just as the daughter was serving drinks to a couple of carters.

'Her eyes were red. She didn't dare look at us. The old woman came back. There was another parley at the back of the building.

'When the father returned, he had that look on his face that you've seen for yourself.

'It was only later that I understood the reason for all their comings and goings. The two women had found Joseph Heurtin in the outhouse and decided not to tell the old man.

'He sensed that there was something going on ... After his wife went out, he questioned his daughter, who couldn't keep her mouth shut ... So off he went to see our man but not before making it plain he wasn't going to have him in the house.

'You've seen him. He's a decent man and probably has strict principles ... And then the penny dropped about who I was ...

'I don't think he would have handed his boy over to me ... Maybe he'd even decided to help him get away

'Be that as it may, around ten o'clock, when I happened to be standing by the window that gives on to the yard, I saw the old girl picking her way along in the lee of the walls as she headed towards the outhouse.

'A matter of seconds later she was yelling blue murder! It wasn't a pretty sight, sir. I got there at the same time as old man Heurtin and I swear I saw sweat pouring out of him . . .

'Our man was slumped at an odd angle against the wall, and you had to look closely before you realized that he had hanged himself from a nail . . .

'The old man had more presence of mind than I did. It was he who cut the rope. He laid his son on his back on the straw and started pulling his tongue, giving him artificial respiration and shouting to his daughter to go and fetch the doctor.

'Since then it's all been a shambles . . . You saw . . . My throat still feels tight . . .

'Nobody in Nandy knows what's happened . . . They all think it's the old woman who's been taken ill . . .

'Between the two of us, we carried the body upstairs, and the doctor's been seeing to him for the last half hour . . .

'Apparently Joseph Heurtin could pull through . . . His father hasn't spoken a word. The daughter's had hysterics, and they've shut her up in the kitchen to stop her screaming.'

A door opened. Maigret stepped out on to the landing and saw the doctor, who was getting ready to leave.

He went downstairs behind him and halted him in the bar.

'Police Judiciaire, doctor . . . How is he?'

He was a country doctor and did not hide his dislike of the police.

'Are you going to march him off?' he asked bad-temperedly.

'I don't know. What state is he in?'

'He was cut down just in time. But it'll take him a few days yet to get over it. Was it at the Santé that he was allowed to get so weak? You'd think he had no blood left in his veins.'

'I must ask you not to discuss this with anyone.'

'There's no need to ask. There's such a thing as professional duty of confidentiality.'

The old man had also come downstairs. His eyes were fixed on the inspector. But he asked no questions. Out of habit he picked up the two empty glasses which stood on the counter and dipped them in the sink.

It was a moment charged with repressed anguish. The sobbing of the girl reached the three men. In the end, Maigret gave a sigh.

'Would you like to keep him here for a time?' he asked as he watched the old man.

There was no answer.

'I'll have to leave one of my officers here in the house.'

The old innkeeper's eyes dwelled on Lucas and then he lowered them again and stared at the counter. A tear rolled down one cheek.

'He swore to his mother . . .' he began.

But he looked away. He could not speak. To hide his

discomfiture he poured himself a glass of rum but as he put it to his lips he retched.

Maigret turned to Lucas but merely said:

'Stay here.'

He did not leave straight away. He walked along the corridor and found a door which opened on to the inner courtyard. Through the kitchen windows he saw the figure of a woman leaning against a wall, her head in her folded arms.

On the further side of the dung-heap, the outhouse door was wide open, and a length of rope was still dangling from an iron nail.

He gave a shrug, walked back the way he had come and found Lucas, who was now the only occupant of the bar.

'Where is he?'

'Upstairs.'

'Did he say anything? Look, I'll send someone to relieve you . . . I want you to ring me twice a day . . .'

'It was you! It was all your fault, you're the one who killed him!' sobbed the old woman on the floor above. 'Get out! . . . You killed him! . . . My boy . . . My lovely boy! . . .'

The bell jangled at the end of its bracket. Maigret himself answered the door and then left to get back into the taxi, which was waiting at the edge of the village.

8. A Man in the House

When Maigret emerged from the taxi outside the Henderson villa at Saint-Cloud, it was just after three in the afternoon. On the way back from Nandy it had struck him that he had forgotten to return to Mrs Henderson's American heirs the key which he had been given in the previous July to enable him to carry out his inquiries.

He went back now with no particular object in mind, with half a hope that chance might lead him to something he had overlooked, or even more, with the idea that the atmosphere might give him inspiration.

The main building, which was surrounded by a garden too small to be called grounds, was enormous, but without style, and ornamented with a turret in appalling taste.

All the shutters were closed. The paths were covered with dead leaves.

The gate in the railings swung open. Maigret felt slightly uneasy in these surroundings, which were so forbidding that they put him in mind more of a cemetery than a home.

He climbed heavily up the four front steps, which were flanked by pretentious plaster figures each topped with a branched electric lamp, opened the main door and was obliged to wait a moment until his eyes got used to the gloom.

There was a disturbing feel to the place, for it was both luxurious and run down. The ground floor had not been in use for four years, that is, since the death of Mr Henderson.

But most of the furniture and furnishings were just as they had been. When Maigret entered the drawing room, for example, the crystal chandelier tinkled softly, and the boards of the wooden floor creaked as he walked over them.

Out of curiosity, he tried the light switch. Ten out of twelve lamps came on. The bulbs were so thickly encrusted with dust that their light was dimmed.

In one corner were valuable carpets which had been rolled up. The armchairs had been pushed to the far end of the room, and assorted travelling trunks had ended up there in no particular order. One was empty. Another still contained some of the dead man's clothes, with mothballs sprinkled over them. Yet he had been deceased for more than four years! The house had been accustomed to stylish living. In this very room there had been receptions which had been reported in the press.

In full view on the enormous mantelpiece was a half-opened box of Havanas.

It was probably at this spot that the visitor had the clearest impression of just how overwhelming the house was.

Mrs Henderson was almost seventy when she had been widowed.

She had been too fatigued to make the effort to organize a new life for herself.

She had settled for shutting herself away in her rooms and had left the rest to go to seed.

They had probably been happy together; at any rate they had made a brilliant couple and had cut a figure in most of the world's capitals.

And all that had been left of it was an old woman shut away with her companion!

And one night, that old lady . . .

Maigret walked through two other reception rooms, then a dining room and emerged at the foot of a great staircase with steps which, up to the first floor, were made of marble.

The faintest sounds reverberated in the absolute silence of the house.

The Crosbys had not touched anything. It was even possible that after their aunt's funeral they had never been back.

The house had been completely neglected, to the point where on the carpet the inspector found a candle he had used during his original investigation.

When he reached the first-floor landing, he suddenly stopped, aware of a certain uneasiness which it took him a moment to analyse. Then he held his breath and listened hard.

Had he heard something? He wasn't sure. But for one reason or another, he'd had a feeling that he was not alone in the house. He seemed to sense, as it were, a stirring of life. At first he gave a shrug. But just as he was opening a door directly facing him, he frowned and simultaneously began breathing more quickly.

A smell of tobacco smoke had reached his nostrils.

Someone had been smoking in the room only moments before. Maybe that someone still was?

He took a few quick paces forwards and found himself in the dead woman's dressing room. The door to the bedroom was half open, but when he went through it he saw nothing. On the other hand, the smell of smoke was stronger here. Moreover there was fine cigarette ash on the floor.

'Who's there?'

He would have liked to be less uneasy but though he tried he could not fight the feeling. Didn't it look as if everything was joining forces to unsettle him?

Hardly any attempt had been made to clear up traces of the carnage from the bedroom. A dress belonging to Mrs Henderson was still draped over the easy chair. The venetian blinds allowed only uniform bars of light to filter through.

But in that atmospheric gloom someone moved.

For a sound had come from the bathroom, a metallic noise. Maigret leaped forwards, saw no one, then heard, distinctly this time, the sound of footsteps on the other side of the door of a lumber room.

His hand automatically felt the pocket where he kept his revolver. He hurled himself at the door, ran through the room and saw a back stairway.

Here it was lighter because the windows overlooking the Seine were not fitted with venetian blinds.

Someone was climbing the stairs and trying to muffle the sounds of his footsteps. Again Maigret called:

'Who's there?'

His excitement was growing. Would it turn out that he'd find all the answers when he was least expecting to?

He started to run. A door slammed on the floor above. The intruder was running away, charging through one room then opening and closing the door of the next.

But Maigret was gaining on him. As on the ground floor, these rooms, which had been used by guests, had been left to fester. They were cluttered with furniture and all kinds of jumble.

A vase was knocked to the floor with a crash. Maigret was afraid of only one thing: that he would come up against a door which the intruder had had time to bolt shut.

'Stop! Police!' he shouted. It was worth a try.

But the man kept on running. He had now covered half the length of the second floor. At one point, Maigret was actually holding a door knob while the intruder's hand was trying to turn the key in the lock on the other side of the door.

'Open up or . . . !'

The key turned. The bolt was pushed home. Without even stopping a moment to think, Maigret took several steps back and hurled himself forward, putting his shoulder to the panel of the door.

It shook but did not give. From the room on the other side came the sound of a window opening.

'Stop! Police!'

He was not thinking that his presence here, in this house which now belonged to William Crosby, was illegal, since he did not have a search warrant.

Two, three times he launched himself against the door. One of the panels started to split.

As he was about to gather his forces for one last attempt, there was a shot followed by a silence so absolute that Maigret stood where he was with his mouth half open as if frozen to the spot.

'Who's in there? Open this door!'

Nothing! No dying groan! Not even the tell-tale sound of a gun being cocked to be fired again.

Overcome by a rush of anger, Maigret battered the door with his shoulder and the whole of his side, and suddenly it gave, so suddenly that his momentum carried him into the room, where he almost went sprawling on the floor.

Cold, damp air was blowing in to the room through the open window, through which the illuminated windows of a restaurant and the yellow bulk of a tram were visible.

On the floor a man was sitting, with his back to the wall and leaning slightly to his left.

The patch of grey which was made by his clothes and the outline of his body were enough for Maigret to recognize William Crosby. It would have been difficult to identify him by his face.

For the American had fired a bullet into his mouth, at point-blank range. Half his head was missing.

*

As he went back slowly through all the rooms he had come through, Maigret switched on the lights. Some lamps had no bulbs, but against all expectations most were still working.

He continued until half the house was lit from top to bottom, with a few black gaps here and there.

When he reached Mrs Henderson's room, he noticed that there was a phone on a bedside table. He lifted the receiver, on the off chance, but a click informed him that the line had not been cut off.

He had never before felt so strongly that he was in a house of death.

Was he not sitting on the edge of the very bed in which an elderly American widow had been murdered? Straight ahead of him he could see the door behind which the body of her maid had been found.

And upstairs, in a mouldering room, there was a new corpse lying under a window which let in the rain-laden evening air.

'Operator? Préfecture, please.'

He spoke in a whisper, though he was not aware of doing so.

'Hello? . . . Give me the head of the Police Judiciaire . . . It's Maigret . . . Ah, is that you, sir? . . . William Crosby has just killed himself in the villa out at Saint-Cloud . . . Yes, I'm still here . . . I'm at the scene . . . Will you do the necessary? I was there! . . . Less than four metres from him . . . There was a locked door between us . . . I know . . . No I can't explain . . . Maybe later . . .'

When he had hung up, he remained motionless for a few minutes, staring straight in front of him.

With his mind elsewhere, he started slowly filling a pipe, which he then forgot to light.

To him the villa felt like a large, empty, cold box, in which he was an insignificant nobody.

'Falsified facts . . .' he managed to say in a murmur.

He almost went back upstairs. But what was the point? The American could not be more dead . . . His right hand was still gripping the automatic with which he had killed himself.

Maigret smiled at the thought that at that very moment Coméliau was being informed of this latest turn of events. It would most likely be he who would turn up in person with men and the experts from Criminal Records.

On the wall hung a large portrait in oils of Mr Henderson looking dignified in evening dress, wearing the sash of the Légion d'honneur and various foreign decorations.

The inspector started walking and went into the next room, which had belonged to Élise Chatrier. He opened a wardrobe. Inside were a number of black dresses, some silk, others linen, which had been neatly hung up.

He listened out for sounds coming from outside. He gave a sigh of relief when he heard two cars pull up more or less simultaneously outside the main gate. Then there were voices in the garden. Monsieur Coméliau was saying in his usual hectoring tones, which made his voice sound over-shrill:

'I never heard the like! It's unacceptable!'

Maigret made his way to the landing, rather like a host

preparing to receive his guests. As soon as the door down-stairs opened he called:

'This way . . .'

Later he would remember how the examining magis-trate suddenly burst in, gave him a fierce look, his lips trembling with indignation, and finally managed to spit out:

'I'm waiting to hear what you have to say for yourself, detective chief inspector!'

Maigret merely turned and led the way up the service stairs and through the bedrooms on the second floor.

'There . . .'

'Did you arrange to meet him here?'

'I didn't even know he was anywhere near! I came on the off chance, to satisfy myself I hadn't missed anything.'

'Where was he?'

'Probably in his aunt's bedroom. He ran off, and I went after him . . . We reached this room, and as I was breaking the door down he killed himself.'

Judging by the way Coméliau looked at him, anyone would have thought that he suspected Maigret of making up the entire story. In reality, it was only because the mag-istrate hated complications.

The pathologist was examining the corpse. Cameras were being pointed everywhere.

'And Heurtin?' barked Coméliau.

' . . . will be returned to his cell in the Santé whenever you want.'

'You've located him?'

Maigret shrugged.

'So let's have him back at once, shall we?'

'As you wish, sir.'

'Is that all you have for me?'

'For the moment.'

'And do you still think that . . . ?'

'. . . that Heurtin didn't kill anybody? I really don't know. I asked you to give me ten days. I've had only four.'

'Where are you going now?'

'No idea.'

Maigret buried his hands deep in his pockets, watched the officers of the prosecutor's office going about their tasks and then suddenly rushed down to Mrs Henderson's bedroom and picked up the phone.

'Hello? Hôtel Georges V? Could you tell me if Madame Crosby is there? . . . Say again? . . . In the salon de thé? Thanks . . . No! . . . No message.'

Monsieur Coméliau, who had followed him down and was by the door, watched him with unfriendly eyes.

'You see what complications . . .'

Maigret did not answer, jammed his hat on his head and, with a curt nod, left the building. He had not told the taxi which had brought him to wait and he was obliged to walk all the way to the bridge at Saint-Cloud before he found another.

Muted music playing. Couples dancing listlessly. Groups of pretty women, especially foreigners, sitting around the tables in the discreet surroundings of the salon de thé of the Hôtel Georges V.

Maigret, who had not surrendered his overcoat at

the cloakroom without grumbling bad-temperedly, approached one group, in which he had recognized Edna Reichberg and Mrs Crosby.

They were in the company of a young man who looked Scandinavian. He seemed to be telling them very funny stories because they laughed all the time.

'Madame Crosby,' said Maigret, with a polite nod.

She looked at him curiously then turned back to her companions with the surprised air of one who was not expecting to be disturbed.

'I'm listening . . .'

'Might I have a word with you?'

'What, now? What is it about?'

But he looked so solemn that she got to her feet and looked around for a quiet spot.

'Come to the bar. There's no one there at this time of day.'

The bar was in fact quite deserted. The two of them remained standing.

'Did you know that your husband intended to go out to Saint-Cloud this afternoon?'

'I don't understand. He is perfectly free to . . .'

'What I'm asking is did he mention that he was intending to visit the villa?'

'No.'

'Have the two of you been there since the death of . . .'

She answered no with a shake of her head.

'Never! It's too upsetting.'

'Your husband went there today by himself.'

She began to be anxious and looked impatiently at the inspector.

'And?'

'There's been an accident.'

'His car, I assume. I'd have bet . . .'

Edna walked past out of curiosity, giving them an inquisitive look, and said by way of an excuse that she was looking for her handbag, which she had left somewhere.

'No, madame. Your husband tried to end his life.'

The young woman's eyes suddenly filled with astonishment then doubt. For a brief instant she was perhaps about to burst out laughing.

'William . . . ?'

'He shot himself with a revolver in the . . .'

And then two hands were urgently gripping Maigret's wrists as Mrs Crosby began questioning him animatedly in English.

Then she gave a great shudder, let go of the inspector and took one step backwards.

'I am sorry, madame, to have to inform you that your husband died two hours ago in the villa at Saint-Cloud.'

She lost interest in him. She strode quickly through the salon de thé without looking at either Edna or her companion, hurried into the lobby and, hatless and empty-handed, went out into the street.

The doorman asked her:

'May I get you a taxi?'

But she had already got into a cab and was telling the driver:

'Saint-Cloud! And hurry . . . !'

Maigret did not follow her but retrieved his coat from

the cloakroom and, seeing a passing bus which was heading towards the Cité, he jumped on to the platform.

'Anyone phone for me?' he asked, pausing to speak to the office clerk.

'About two o'clock . . . There's a note on your desk.'

The note read:

Call from Inspector Janvier to Detective Chief Inspector Maigret. A fitting at his tailor's. Lunch in restaurant on Boulevard Montparnasse. At two, Radek goes to Coupole for coffee. Makes two phone calls.

And since two in the afternoon?

Maigret sank into his chair after turning the key in the lock of his office door. He was very surprised to wake up with a start when his watch said ten-thirty.

'Has anyone been on the phone asking for me?'

'Oh, were you there all the time? I thought you'd gone out. Monsieur Coméliau rang twice . . .'

'How about Janvier?'

'No.'

Half an hour later, Maigret walked into the bar of the Coupole and looked round without success for Radek and the inspector. He took the bartender to one side.

'Has the Czech been in?'

'He showed his face this afternoon. He was with your colleague. You know, the young one in the mackintosh.'

'Were they at the same table?'

'They sure were, in that corner. They drank at least four whiskies apiece.'

'When did they leave?'

'First they ate in the brasserie.'

'Together?'

'Together. They must have left around ten.'

'You don't happen to know where they went?'

'Ask the doorman. He called the taxi for them.'

The doorman remembered them:

'Hold on! It was that blue taxi – he usually parks here
. . . They can't have gone far because he's there, he's back
already.'

The next moment, the taxi-driver was saying:

'The last fare? I drove them to the Pelican, Rue des
Écoles.'

'Take me there!'

Maigret walked into the Pelican in the foulest of moods,
put the doorman in his place and then the waiter who tried
to show him into the main hall.

Among the crowd of good-time girls and revellers milling around the bar, he spotted the two men he was
looking for perched on high bar stools in a corner.

It took him only a glance to see that Janvier's eyes were
shining and his face over-excited.

Radek on the other hand was staring grim-faced into his
glass.

Without hesitating, Maigret went straight up to them,
while Janvier, patently drunk, made signs which meant:
'All in hand! . . . Leave everything to me! . . . Don't show
your face!'

He stood next to the two men. The Czech, slow-
tongued, murmured:

'Aha! It's you again!'

Janvier was still making signs in a way which he believed was both discreet and eloquent.

'What will you have to drink, inspector?'

'Look, Radek . . .'

'Bartender! Same again for my friend here!'

And the Czech swallowed the concoction he had in the glass in front of him and sighed:

'I'm listening . . . And you're listening too, aren't you, Janvier?'

At the same time he thumped the young inspector on the back:

'Is it long since you've been to Saint-Cloud?' said Maigret slowly and clearly.

'Me? . . . Ha ha ha! . . . That's a good one!'

'You know there's another corpse?'

'Gravediggers are doing good business, then. Your very good health, inspector.'

He wasn't playing games. He was drunk, certainly not as drunk as Janvier, but even so he had had more than enough to be glassy-eyed and for him to hang on to the bar rail.

'And who is the lucky man?'

'William Crosby.'

For the space of a few seconds, Radek seemed to be fighting against his drunkenness, as if he had suddenly realized the gravity of the moment.

Then he gave a derisive laugh as he straightened himself up, leaned back and made a sign to the barman to refill their glasses.

'Well now, isn't that just one in the eye for you!'

'And what does that mean?'

'You're nowhere near, man! . . . In fact, further away than ever! . . . I told you from the start . . . So now let me make a useful suggestion. Janvier and I, we're both agreed . . . Your job is to follow me. Actually, I don't give a damn! Only instead of walking like sheep one behind the other playing games, I think it would make more sense if we had a good time together . . . Have you had dinner? . . . In that case, since we never know what tomorrow might bring, I suggest we make a night of it for once . . . This place is full of pretty girls. We'll each pick one. Janvier has already been chatting up that brunette over there . . . I haven't made my mind up yet . . . Naturally it's on me . . .

'So, what do you say?'

He stared at Maigret, who stared back and found no trace of drunkenness in his companion's face.

Instead he saw the same eyes ablaze with acute intelligence which were now fixed on him with a look of consummate irony, as though Radek were truly possessed by fierce exultant joy.

9. The Next Day

It was eight in the morning. Maigret, who had left Radek and Janvier four hours earlier, was drinking black coffee while slowly, with a pause after every sentence, he was writing in a cramped hand:

7 July. At midnight, Joseph Heurtin drinks four glasses of spirits in the Pavillon Bleu in Saint-Cloud and drops a third-class railway ticket.

2.30 a.m. Mrs Henderson and her maid are stabbed to death, and the traces left by the murderer are those of Joseph Heurtin.

4 a.m. Heurtin returns home to Rue Monsieur-le-Prince.

8 July. Heurtin reports for work as usual.

9 July. On the evidence of his shoe-prints he is arrested at his place of work, in Rue de Sèvres. He does not deny going to Saint-Cloud. He says that he has not killed anybody.

2 October. Joseph Heurtin, still protesting his innocence, is sentenced to death.

15 October. He escapes from the Santé prison using the plan devised by the police, wanders through Paris all night and ends up at the Citanguette, where he falls asleep.

16 October. The morning papers carry the story of his escape, without comment. At ten that morning an

unknown hand writes a letter in the Coupole, which is sent to *Le Sifflet* and reveals that the police were complicit in the break-out. The unidentified writer is a man, a foreigner, who writes using his left hand and is probably suffering from some incurable illness.

6 p.m. Heurtin gets up. Inspector Dufour, who tries to take the newspaper he is holding away from him, is hit with a soda siphon. Heurtin makes the most of the confusion, blacks out the room and runs off while the inspector panics and fires a shot but to no avail.

17 October. At 12 noon William Crosby, his wife and Edna Reichberg are drinking aperitifs in the bar of the Coupole, where they are regulars. Radek the Czech is sitting at a table, where he orders café au lait and a yogurt. The Crosbys and Radek do not appear to know each other.

Outside, Heurtin, exhausted and hungry, waits for someone.

The Crosbys leave, and he doesn't turn a hair.

Heurtin goes on waiting *even when Radek is the only one left in the bar*.

5 p.m. The Czech orders caviar, refuses to pay and leaves, escorted by two policemen.

Once he has gone, Heurtin ends his picket and makes his way to his parents' house at Nandy.

That same evening, at around nine o'clock, Crosby changes a 100-dollar bill in the Hôtel Georges V and puts the bundles of French notes in his pocket.

Accompanied by his wife, he attends a charity gala at the Ritz, gets back to his suite around three in the morning and does not go out again.

18 October. At Nandy, Heurtin has crept into an out-house, where his mother finds and hides him.

9 a.m. His father suspects that he is there and orders him to leave once it is dark.

10 a.m. Heurtin tries to commit suicide by hanging himself in the outhouse.

In Paris, Radek is released by the inspector-in-charge at Montparnasse police station at about 7 a.m. He manages to lose Inspector Janvier, who is tailing him, shaves and changes his shirt somewhere, although he does not have a centime in his pocket.

10 a.m. He makes a conspicuous entrance at the Coupole, waves a 1,000-franc note and settles himself down at a table.

A little later, he sees Maigret enter and invites him to sample the caviar and, without any prompting, raises the Henderson case and asserts that the police will never get to the bottom of it.

But no one in the police has ever mentioned the name Henderson in his presence.

Then, quite spontaneously, he lays ten bundles of 100-franc notes on the table and volunteers the information that they are newly minted and therefore easily traceable.

William Crosby, who returned to his hotel at three in the morning, *has at that moment not set foot outside his suite.* Yet these are the same notes as the ones given to him the previous evening by the clerk in the Georges V in exchange for his banknote.

Inspector Janvier remains at the Coupole to keep an eye

on Radek. After lunch, the Czech invites him to have a drink *and makes two phone calls*.

4 p.m. There is a man in the villa at Saint-Cloud, although it has been deserted ever since the funeral of Mrs Henderson and her maid.

The man is William Crosby. He is up on the first floor. He hears the sounds of footsteps in the garden. It is impossible that *he does not recognize Maigret* through the window.

He hides. He runs away as Maigret advances. He climbs up to the second floor. He is forced to retreat room by room and, finally trapped in a room from which there is no exit, he opens the window, sees that there is no escape, puts a gun in his mouth and fires.

Mrs Crosby and Edna Reichberg go dancing in the salon de thé at the Hôtel Georges V.

Radek invites Inspector Janvier to dine with him and then afterwards to have a drink in a bar in the Latin Quarter.

When Maigret catches up with them at 11 p.m., they are drunk and, until 4 a.m., Radek takes great delight in dragging his companions from bar to bar, making them drink, drinking himself and appearing at times drunk and at others lucid, scattering statements which are deliberately ambiguous and repeating that the police will never solve the Henderson case.

4 a.m. He invites two women to his table. He insists that both his companions do likewise and, when they refuse, he goes off with the women to a hotel in Boulevard Saint-Germain.

19 October. At eight in the morning, the hotel's reception desk replies:

'The two women are still asleep. Their friend has just left. He settled the bill in full.'

Maigret was overcome by a weariness such as he had rarely felt during an investigation. He looked cursorily over what he had just written and, without a word, shook the hand of a colleague who had said hello and, with a gesture, indicated that he was to be left to himself.

In the margin, he made a note: 'Ascertain what William Crosby was doing between 11 a.m. and 4 p.m. on 19 October.'

Then suddenly, with a purposeful movement of his head, he picked up the receiver and asked to be put through to the Coupole.

'I want to know how long it's been since the last time correspondence arrived for the name of Radek.'

Five minutes later, he had the answer.

'At least ten days.'

He then asked to speak to the hotel where the Czech had a room.

'About a week,' he was told in response to the same question.

He reached for the phone book, found the list of poste restante offices and rang the one in Boulevard Raspail.

'Do you have someone on your books by the name of Radek? . . . No? . . . He must use his initials only to get his post sent to him . . . Police business . . . Listen, miss . . . He's foreign, quite shabbily dressed, with very long,

curly red hair . . . What was that? . . . The initials M. V.?
. . . When was the last time he got a letter? . . . Yes, please
find out . . . I'll wait . . . No, don't hang up . . .'

There was a knock at the door. Without turning round
he called out:

'Come!

'Yes, still here . . . What's that? Yesterday morning at
nine? . . . And this letter came through the post? . . . Thank
you! . . . Oh, just a moment . . . The letter was quite large,
was it, large enough to contain a bundle of banknotes?'

'You're doing well!' growled a voice behind Maigret.

The inspector turned. The Czech was standing there,
looking forlorn yet with a barely perceptible twinkle in
his eye. As he took a seat, he went on:

'True, it wasn't a very clever thing to do. But now you
know: yesterday morning I collected money that had been
sent to me care of the poste restante in Boulevard Raspail.
The previous evening, the money was in the pocket of the
late lamented Crosby . . . But was it Crosby himself who
sent it? Now there's a question.'

'Did the duty clerk let you in here?'

'He was busy dealing with some woman. I just behaved
as if I work here and saw your name on a door. It wasn't
difficult. And to think that here we are, at the beating heart
of the nation's top police force!'

Maigret observed that his face looked tired, not tired
like the face of a man who has passed a sleepless night,
but like the face of a patient whose illness has just taken
a turn for the worse. There were bags under his eyes. His
lips were bloodless.

'Is there something you want to say to me?'

'I don't know. I mostly wanted to see how you were. Did you get home in one piece last night?'

'Good of you to ask.'

From where he was sitting, he could see the summary Maigret had just written out to clarify his ideas, and the suspicion of a smile flitted over his lips.

'Know anything about the Taylor case?' he asked unexpectedly. 'No, you probably don't keep up with American newspapers. Well, Desmond Taylor, one of Hollywood's best-known directors, was murdered in 1922. At least a dozen film stars, including some pretty women, were suspects. They were all released without charge. Well now, do you have any idea of what is still being said about it, today, after all these years? I'm quoting from memory, but my memory is excellent: *The police have known very well who killed Taylor from the first day of the investigation. But the evidence they have is inadequate and so flimsy that, even if the perpetrator turned himself in, he would have to provide irrefutable evidence himself and call witnesses to back up his story.*'

Maigret stared in amazement at Radek, who crossed his legs, lit a cigarette and continued:

'Now, those words were pronounced by the chief of police in person. And that was a year ago today exactly. I have not forgotten one syllable of it. And it goes without saying, *Taylor's murderer has never been arrested* . . .'

With a show of indifference, Maigret leaned back in his chair, put his feet on the desk and waited with the detached air of one who has all the time in the world but is not particularly interested in the conversation.

'So have you finally decided to make inquiries about William Crosby, then? At the time of the murder, the police never thought of it . . . or maybe they didn't dare . . .'

'Did you come here with information for me?' said Maigret, gritting his teeth.

'Yes, if that's what you want! But anyone in Montparnasse could put you straight about him. First, when his aunt died, he had debts amounting to 600,000 francs, and even Bob at the Coupole was lending him money. It's something that happens regularly with these grand families. He might have been Henderson's nephew but he was never very well off. Another of his uncles is a multi-millionaire. He has a cousin who is director of America's biggest bank. But his father was ruined ten years ago. Have you got the picture? In a word, he was the poor relation.

'And to make it worse, all his uncles and aunts had children – all except the Hendersons.

'So he spent his time waiting for the old man to die and then after him Mrs Henderson. Both of them were in their seventies.

'So, what do you reckon to that?'

'Nothing.'

Maigret's silence clearly exasperated the Czech.

'You know as well as I do that in Paris a man who has a name which carries a certain cachet can get by perfectly well without money. Crosby was also a man of great charm. He'd never done a day's work in his life. Actually, he was just like a great big kid, happy to be alive and sample everything . . .

'Especially women! . . . He was nice to them . . . You've seen Madame Crosby. He was very much in love with her.

'Even so . . . Fortunately, those who are in the know about these sorts of things stick together closer than freemasons . . . I'd see the two of them having an aperitif at the Coupole and a girl hanging around who'd make a sign to William . . .

'"Do you mind, darling? . . . There's something I must do. It's just round the corner . . ."

'And everybody there knew that he was going to spend half an hour in the first hotel you come to in Rue Delambre.

'And that happened not once but many times. It also goes without saying that Edna Reichberg was his mistress, while all the time spending every day with Madame Crosby and being nice to her . . . And there were lots more of them! . . .

'He could never say no to women. I really believe he loved them all.'

Maigret yawned and stretched.

'Or again there were times when he didn't have his taxi fare home yet he would buy rounds of fifteen cocktails for people he hardly knew. And he was always laughing. I never saw him worried about anything . . . You have to imagine a man who was born with a sunny temperament, someone whom everybody loves, who loves everybody, who is forgiven everything, even those things for which no one should ever be forgiven . . . And with it a man who succeeds at everything! . . . Are you a gambler? Then you won't know what it's like to see your opponent draw a seven and you turn your cards over and you have drawn an eight? And in the next hand, he draws eight and you get nine! Time after time! As if it was happening, not in the realm of tawdry real life, but in the land of dreams!

'Well, that was Crosby!

'When he inherited fifteen, sixteen million, he was sailing close to the wind because I think he forged the signatures of several illustrious members of his family to pay off debts.'

'But he killed himself,' barked Maigret.

The Czech laughed to himself. It could have meant anything. He stood up so that he could drop his cigarette end into the coal-scuttle then returned to his seat.

'But it was *only yesterday* that he killed himself,' he said enigmatically.

'Hold it there!'

All at once Maigret's tone was peremptory. He was now on his feet and staring at Radek, looking him up and down.

There was a moment of almost painful silence before Maigret said:

'Why the hell did you come here?'

'For a chat. Or if you prefer, to give you a helping hand. You must admit that you'd have taken some time to get the information about Crosby that I've just handed to you . . . Would you like more of the same, equally genuine?

'You've seen the little Reichberg girl. She's twenty. Well, she's been William's mistress for a year and during that time she was spending every day with Madame Crosby, with whom she's been very lovey-dovey . . .

'And all the time she and her lover-boy have had an

understanding that Crosby will get a divorce and marry her . . .

'But if William was going to marry the daughter of the rich industrialist Reichberg, he would need money, lots of money . . .

'What else do you want? Information about Bob, the barman at the Coupole? You've seen him in his white jacket with a serviette over his arm . . .

'Well, he earns four or five hundred thousand francs a year and owns a magnificent villa at Versailles and a luxury car . . . God, that amounts to a lot of tips!'

Radek was starting to get excited. There was something strange, something edgy in his voice.

'And during all that time, Joseph Heurtin was earning 600 francs a month pushing his three-wheeled carrier around Paris for ten or twelve hours a day!'

'And what were you doing?'

The words came out bluntly while Maigret looked directly into the Czech's eyes.

'Me? I . . .'

The two men fell silent. Maigret started striding up and down his office, pausing only to put more coal in the stove. Radek meanwhile lit another cigarette.

The situation was bizarre. It was difficult to see quite what the visitor had come for. He showed no sign of wanting to leave. On the contrary, he seemed to be waiting for something.

Maigret was in no hurry to satisfy his curiosity by asking questions. Besides, what would he have asked him?

It was Radek who spoke first, or rather muttered:

'The perfect crime! . . . I mean the murder of Desmond Taylor, the film director. He was alone in his hotel bedroom. A young starlet pays him a visit. And after that, he is never seen again alive. Are you following? On the other hand, the starlet in question is observed leaving his room without being shown out by him. But she wasn't the one who killed him!'

He was sitting on the chair which Maigret normally kept for visitors. It was directly under the lamp, which gave a harsh light, almost like the light in a hospital ward.

The Czech's face had never been so intriguing. His forehead was high, battered, much furrowed but not in a way that made him look older.

The mop of red hair struck a note of international bohemian nonconformity, which was reinforced by a shirt with a very low one-piece collar, dark in colour and worn with no tie.

Radek was by no means thin, yet he looked sickly, maybe because his flesh seemed soft, flabby. There was also something unhealthy about those plump lips.

He was beginning to get worked up in a very odd way which a psychologist would have found revealing. No muscle of his face moved but the amperage of his pupils seemed to have been given a sudden boost, which lent his eyes a piercing intensity.

'What will they do with Heurtin?' he asked after full five minutes of silence.

'Guillotine him!' grunted Maigret, with his hands in his trouser pockets.

The amperage was powered up to maximum. Radek gave a short, grating laugh.

'Of course they will! A man who earns 600 francs a month! . . . While we're on that, let's have a bet. I say that when Crosby is buried, both women will turn up in full mourning and they'll weep on each other's necks. I mean Madame Crosby and Edna. What do you say, inspector? . . . Can you even be sure he killed himself?'

He laughed. It was unexpected. Everything about him was unexpected, not least this visit.

'It's so easy to dress up a murder to make it look like suicide. So easy that if at the time it happened I had not been with that nice Inspector Janvier I would have turned myself in, confessed to the crime, just to see what would happen . . . Are you married?'

'And if I am?'

'Nothing . . . But you're a lucky man! A wife. A run-of-the-mill job. The satisfaction of duty done. I expect you go fishing on Sundays. Unless you're a billiard player . . . Speaking personally, I find that quite admirable . . .

'But you've got to start early. You must have a father who has principles and is also fond of billiards.'

'Where did you first come across Joseph Heurtin?'

Maigret had put the question, thinking that he was being very subtle. He'd hardly finished speaking before he was regretting it.

'Where did I come across him? In the papers, like everybody else. Unless . . . God, isn't life complicated! When I think that you're sitting there, listening to me, feeling uncomfortable, watching without being able to make up your mind about me and thinking your job, your fishing afternoons, your billiard sessions are all on the line! At your age! Twenty years of unstinting service. Except that you've been unfortunate enough, for once in your life, to have had an idea and stuck to it. It's what you might call a mild attack of genius. As if you had not been touched by genius when you were a baby. I mean, it doesn't suddenly come over you when you're forty-five! . . . That must be near enough your age, no?

'You should have allowed Heurtin to die. You'd have got promotion. Ah yes, what does a chief inspector of the Police Judiciaire earn these days? A couple of thousand? Three? Half of what Crosby spent on drinks? . . . And when I say half . . . Another thing, how are they going to explain Crosby's suicide? Woman trouble? Tongues will wag and they'll link the fact that he shot himself with Heurtin's escape. And all the Crosbys and the Hendersons and the cousins and second cousins who are all big noises in America will be sending wires calling for discretion . . .

'Now, if I were in your place . . .'

He in turn stood up and stubbed out his cigarette on the sole of his shoe.

'If I were you, inspector, I'd look around for a diversionary tactic. Got it! I would, for example, arrest a man about whom no one will need to tread carefully. Someone like Radek, whose mother was a servant in a small town in Czechoslovakia . . . Do Parisians actually know where Czechoslovakia is?'

His voice shook involuntarily. It was rare that his foreign accent was so pronounced.

'But it will all end up like the Taylor case! . . . If I had the time . . . In the Taylor case, for instance, there were no fingerprints or any other such evidence . . . Whereas here . . . Heurtin left traces everywhere and even showed his face in Saint-Cloud! Crosby, who needed money whatever the cost, and then shot himself just as the investigation was being re-opened! . . . Finally, there's me. What am I supposed to have done? I never spoke a word to Crosby. He didn't even know my name. He had never met me. And just you ask Heurtin if he ever heard of Radek! Ask around Saint-Cloud if anybody there ever laid eyes on anyone who looked like me! . . . And yet here I am, in the nerve centre of the Police Judiciaire! . . . There's an inspector waiting for me downstairs to follow me wherever I go . . . Incidentally, will that still be Janvier? . . . I'd like that. He's young. He's a decent sort. He has no head for drink . . . Three cocktails and he's floating on air . . .

'But tell me, inspector, who should a person apply to to make a donation of several thousand francs to the home for superannuated policemen?'

With a careless gesture, he produced a bundle of banknotes from one pocket, put it back, took a second bundle from another pocket, then began his little game again with his waistcoat pocket.

He continued like this until he had displayed a minimum of 100,000 francs.

'Is that all you've got to say?'

It was Radek who spoke the words to Maigret in a tone of vexation which he was unable to disguise.

'That's all.'

'Inspector, would you like me to tell you something?'

No reply.

'In that case, you'll never understand anything!'

He reached for his black fedora, walked stiffly to the door clearly in the foulest of tempers, while Maigret muttered under his breath:

'Sing away, birdie! Sing away! . . .'

10. A Cupboard with a Surprise

'How much do you earn selling papers?'

The scene was a terrace outside a Montparnasse café. Radek, tilted back on his chair and with that smile, which was more sinister than ever, was smoking a Havana.

A poor old woman was moving among the tables holding out evening newspapers to customers, muttering her barely comprehensible solicitations. She was a pitiful, absurd figure.

'How much do I . . . ?'

She did not understand, and the blank look in her eyes was proof that the years had left her only the feeblest glimmer of intelligence.

'Sit yourself down . . . You're going to have a drink with me . . . Waiter! A grog for the lady!'

Radek looked around him for Maigret, who, he knew, was sitting just a few metres away.

'Right, I'll begin by buying all your papers. You'd better count them . . .'

The old woman was flustered and didn't know whether to do as she was told or leave. But the Czech waved a 100-franc note at her, and she began feverishly counting her newspapers.

'Drink up! There are forty, you say? At five sous a go . . .

But wait a minute, would you like to earn another hundred francs?'

Maigret, who could see and hear everything, did not react, He did not even look as if he had noticed what was going on.

'Two hundred francs ... Three hundred ... Just one moment ... Here's your money ... Wait a second: would you like five hundred? But to earn it you must sing a song ... Hands off! Song first ...'

'What do you want me to sing?'

It was all too much for the witless old girl. A drop of liqueur ran stickily down her chin, which was stubbled with grey hairs. Customers sitting at nearby tables nudged each other with their elbows.

'Sing whatever you like. Make it something cheerful. And if you dance, there'll be an extra hundred francs for you.'

It was painful to watch. The wretched old girl did not take her eyes off the banknotes. And as she started humming an unrecognizable tune in a cracked voice, her hand reached for the money.

'Stop it!' said the other customers.

'Sing!' ordered Radek.

He was still keeping an eye open for Maigret. More protests were made. A waiter approached the woman and ordered her to leave. She refused to go, clinging to the hope of earning fabulous wealth.

'I'm singing for this young gent ... He promised me ...'

The end was more odious still. A policeman arrived and

marched the old woman away. She had not seen a penny of the money. A junior waiter ran after her to give her back her newspapers.

There had been a dozen scenes of this sort in the past three days. For those three days, Maigret, beetle-browed, grim-mouthed, had been following Radek wherever he went, from morning to night and night to morning.

At first, the Czech had tried to take up the conversation where it had left off. He had repeated:

'Since you are so determined not to let me out of your sight, why don't we go everywhere together? It would be so much more amusing.'

Maigret had refused. At the Coupole and elsewhere, he would sit at a table near Radek's. In the street, he walked conspicuously close behind him.

Radek was losing patience. It was a war of nerves.

The funeral of William Crosby had taken place, bringing together two very different worlds: the most glitzy ranks of the American colony in Paris and the motley crew from Montparnasse.

As Radek had predicted, both women wore deep mourning. The Czech himself had followed the funeral procession to the cemetery without turning a hair and without exchanging a word with anyone.

Three days of a life so unlikely that it started to feel like a nightmare.

Radek would sometimes turn to Maigret and repeat:

'All this carry-on won't help you to understand any of it!'

The inspector pretended not to hear and remained as

impassive as a blank wall. It was only once or twice that the Czech had even managed to catch his eye.

He just followed him around, that was the top and bottom of it! He didn't appear to be looking for anything in particular. He was a monstrous presence, dogged and permanently *there*.

Radek spent every morning in cafés, doing nothing. Suddenly he would summon a waiter:

'Call the manager!'

And when the manager appeared:

'I would like you to confirm that the waiter who has been serving me has dirty hands.'

He invariably paid with 100- or 1,000-franc notes and stuffed the change in one or other of his pockets.

In restaurants, he would send back dishes which were not to his taste. One day, for lunch, he ate a meal costing 150 francs and then told the waiter:

'There's no tip. You weren't attentive enough!'

In the evening, he would hang around bars and nightclubs, buying drinks for the girls, keeping them on tenterhooks until the last minute, when he would suddenly throw a 1,000-franc note into the middle of the floor and say:

'The girl who gets it keeps it!'

A fight would follow, and some girl would be ejected from the premises while Radek, as usual, would try to work out the effect the incident was having on Maigret.

He never tried to escape the surveillance to which he was being subjected. If he took a taxi, he would wait until the inspector had also hailed one.

*

The funeral was held on 22 October. On the 23rd, at eleven at night, Radek was finishing his dinner in a restaurant just off the Champs Élysées.

At eleven-thirty, he left, followed by Maigret, carefully selected a comfortable taxi and gave the address to the driver in a whisper.

Two cabs were soon driving one behind the other in the direction of Auteuil. On the policeman's heavy face the casual observer would not have detected any sign of anxiety, impatience or weariness, even though he had not slept for four days.

Except that his eyes were slightly more fixed and staring than usual.

The first taxi followed the Left Bank, crossed the Seine over Pont Mirabeau and took a route that led circuitously to the Citanguette.

Five hundred metres short of the bar, Radek stopped the car, said a few words to the driver and, with both hands in his pockets, set off on foot towards the unloading wharf directly opposite the bar.

There he sat down on a mooring bollard, lit a cigarette, made sure that Maigret had followed him and then remained perfectly still.

By midnight, nothing had happened. In the bar, three Arabs were playing dice, and a man was dozing in one corner, probably fuddled with drink. The landlord was washing wine glasses. There was no light upstairs.

At five minutes after midnight, a taxi drove along the road and stopped outside the front of the bar, and, after a brief hesitation, the figure of a woman ran quickly inside

Radek's sardonic eye kept an even keener lookout for Maigret than ever. The woman was lit by the naked light-bulb. She was wearing a black coat and a wide tippet of some kind of dark fur. Even so it was impossible not to recognize Ellen Crosby.

She was now leaning over the counter, talking quietly to the landlord. The Arabs had paused in their game to watch.

From outside, their voices could not be heard. But there was no doubt about the landlord's stupefied reaction and the American woman's nervous state.

Moments later, the man made his way to the bottom of the staircase behind his counter. She followed him. Then a light appeared in a first-floor window, the window of the room which Joseph Heurtin had occupied when he was on the run.

When the landlord came down again, he was alone. The Arabs called out to him, and as he answered he gave a shrug of his shoulders which very probably meant: 'I don't understand it either! Anyway, it's none of our business!'

There were no shutters on the first floor. The curtains were thin, and it was possible to follow more or less all the American's comings and goings inside.

'Cigarette, inspector?'

Maigret did not answer. In the upstairs room, the young woman had moved to the side of the bed and was stripping the sheets and blankets off it.

They saw her lift some shapeless, heavy object. Then she embarked on some strange activity, became agitated and then suddenly moved to the window as if she had suddenly become worried by something.

'Seems like she has it in for the mattress, wouldn't you say? Either I'm very mistaken or she's ripping it open. An odd thing to do for a woman who has always had a maid!'

Both men were sitting barely five metres apart. A quarter of an hour ticked by.

'It's all getting more and more complicated, don't you think?'

The Czech's impatience could be heard in his voice. Maigret took good care neither to respond nor to react.

It was almost half past midnight when Ellen Crosby reappeared in the bar of the café. She tossed a note on the counter, turned up her fur tippet as she left and hurried to the taxi, which had been waiting for her.

'Shall we follow her, inspector?'

All three taxis set off, one behind the other. But Mrs Crosby was not going to Paris, and half an hour later they were all at Saint-Cloud. She left her taxi near the villa.

She seemed so small as she walked along the pavement on the opposite side of the road, like someone who is not sure about something.

Suddenly, she crossed the road, searched in her handbag for a key and a moment later she was inside, while the gate swung shut behind her with a dull thud.

The lights did not come on. The only sign of life was a faint, intermittent glimmer in the rooms on the first floor, as if someone was striking a match at intervals.

The night was cool. The street lamps lining the road were fogged by a halo of dampness.

The two taxis, one Maigret's, the other Radek's, had stopped 200 metres from the villa, while Mrs Crosby's was parked, by itself, just by the gate.

Maigret had got out of his and was walking up and down, with his hands thrust deeply in his pockets, puffing fretfully on his pipe.

'Well? Aren't you going to see what's going on?'

He did not reply but carried on pacing monotonously to and fro.

'Maybe you're making a mistake, inspector! What if another corpse is found in there later on or tomorrow?'

Maigret did not flinch, and Radek threw down his cigarette, which was only half smoked, after snagging the paper with a fingernail.

'How many times have I told you that you'll never understand this case . . . ? And I'll say it again: you'll . . .'

The inspector turned his back on him. And then almost an hour went by. It had gone quiet. Not even the flickering flame of matches showed in the windows of the villa.

Mrs Crosby's driver started to get anxious. He got out of his seat and was almost at the gate.

'Suppose, inspector, that there's someone else in the villa.'

Maigret turned and looked Radek straight in the eye in such a way that decided him to stay silent.

When, moments later, Ellen Crosby ran out and jumped into her cab, she was holding something in her hand, an object thirty centimetres long wrapped in white paper or a piece of cloth.

'Aren't you curious to know what . . . ?'

'Listen, Radek . . .'

'What?'

The American's taxi was fast disappearing in the direction of Paris. Maigret gave no sign that he was anxious to follow.

The Czech was jumpy. His lips moved, trembling slightly.

'Do you think we should go inside too?'

'But . . .'

He hesitated. He had the air of a man who has worked out a scheme and suddenly finds himself faced with an unexpected hitch.

Maigret laid a heavy hand on his shoulder.

'And now we're going to understand everything, the two of us. Ready?'

Radek laughed. But the laugh was half-hearted.

'Can't make up your mind? Are you afraid, as you said a while back, that you might find yourself dealing with another dead body? . . . Well now, who could that be, I wonder. Madame Henderson is dead and buried, and her maid is also dead and buried. Crosby is dead and buried, and his wife has just left, alive and kicking. And Joseph Heurtin is snug and safe in the sick bay of the Santé prison. Who's left? Edna? But what would she be doing here?'

'After you,' growled Radek through gritted teeth

'Right, we'll start at the beginning. Before we can get into the house, we'll need a key . . .'

But it was not a key that Maigret took out of his pocket but a small cardboard box, which it took him some time to open and from which he eventually extracted the key to the gate.

'There we are! Now all we have to do is go in as if we

were walking into our own house, because there isn't anybody inside . . . Isn't that the truth? No one at home?'

How had this sudden change in him come about? And why? Radek had stopped looking sarcastically at his companion but was staring at him with a degree of apprehension which he could not hide.

'Would you mind keeping this little box in your pocket? We might find a use for it later on . . .'

Maigret turned on the light switch, tapped his pipe on his heel to knock out the ash and then refilled it.

'Let's go upstairs . . . Obviously getting in was as easy for whoever killed Madame Henderson as it is for us. Two sleeping women! No dog! No janitor! And on top of that, carpets everywhere! . . . Come on!'

The inspector did not even bother to try to see what the Czech was doing.

'You were right back there, Radek . . . It would come as a nasty surprise to me if we really did find a body . . . You know Monsieur Coméliau's reputation . . . He's already got it in for me because I didn't prevent Crosby from killing himself, which he did more or less in my presence . . . He's also annoyed with me because I couldn't explain what happened . . .

'So just imagine if there was another murder! . . . What would I say? . . . What could I do? . . . I allowed Madame Crosby to get away . . . And as for you, I could hardly accuse you, since I've not let you out of my sight! . . .

'Indeed, after the last three days, it would be difficult to say which of us has been following the other. Have you been following me? Or have I been following you?'

He seemed to be talking to himself. They had now reached the first floor, and Maigret went straight through the dressing room and into the bedroom where Mrs Henderson had been murdered.

'Come in, Radek . . . I imagine that you are not particularly upset by the thought that two women were killed here? One detail you might perhaps not know. We never found the knife. It was assumed that, as he ran away, Heurtin must have thrown it into the Seine.'

Maigret sat down on the edge of the bed, at the very place where the body of the American woman had been found.

'Want to know what I think? Well, I think the killer hid the knife here. But he hid it so well that that we missed it . . . Wait a moment! . . . Hang on! . . . Did you notice the shape of that parcel which Madame Crosby went off with? . . . Thirty centimetres long and just a few centimetres wide . . . The measurements of a substantial dagger, wouldn't you say? . . . You're quite right, Radek! This is a horribly tangled business! . . . But . . . hello, what have we here?'

He leaned forwards over the polished parquet, where there were fairly clear footprints. They made out a small heel print, the heel of a woman's shoe.

'How is your eyesight? . . . Good, then you can help me to follow these prints . . . Who knows, we might even find out why Madame Crosby came here tonight!'

Radek hesitated, looked closely at Maigret like a man who is wondering what part he is being cast for. But he could not read the expression on the inspector's face.

'The trail leads to the maid's bedroom, right? . . . And then? . . . Bend lower, man . . . Unlike me, you don't yet weigh a hundred kilos! . . . Well? . . . The prints stop in front of this cupboard? . . . Ah, it's a hanging-wardrobe! . . . Is it locked? . . . No! Wait a moment before opening it . . . You mentioned a corpse . . . What do you say? What if there's one inside!'

Radek lit a cigarette. His hands were shaking.

'Come on! We'll have to make up our mind and open it . . . Go at it, man . . .'

And, still talking, Maigret straightened his tie in a mirror, but without once taking his eyes off his companion.

'Well?'

The cupboard door opened:

'Is there a dead body in there? What's the matter?'

Radek had taken three steps back. He was staring with astonishment at a young women with fair hair who now emerged from her hiding-place. She moved somewhat stiffly but was not at all scared.

It was Edna Reichberg.

She looked first at Maigret and then at the Czech as though she was waiting for an explanation. She did not appear in the least concerned.

But she did display the awkwardness of someone who acts a part to which he or she is not accustomed.

Ignoring her entirely, Maigret had turned to Radek, who was trying to regain his composure.

'What have you got to say now? We were expecting a corpse – or rather you led me to think that I was going to find a corpse – and what we get is a charming young woman who is very much alive!'

Edna had turned and was also looking at the Czech.

'Well, Radek?' Maigret went on cheerfully.

Silence.

'Do you still believe that I'll never understand anything? . . . Did you speak? . . .'

The Swedish girl, whose eyes never left Radek, opened her mouth, but the cry of fear died in her throat.

Maigret had turned back to the mirror and was smoothing down his hair with the flat of his hand. Meanwhile, the Czech had pulled a revolver out of his pocket and, taking quick aim, he pulled the trigger at the very instant the girl was vainly trying to scream.

It was a sight as amazing as it was absurd. There was a faint metallic click, like something a child's toy might have made. No bullet was fired. Radek pulled the trigger again.

The rest happened so quickly that Edna did not understand what followed. Maigret had seemed to be solidly planted where he was. Yet, in the space of one second, he pounced and crashed with all his weight into the Czech, sending him sprawling on the floor.

Had he not said: 'A hundred kilos!'?

And, making full use of his bulk, he overpowered his opponent, who, after two or three attempts to break free, lay still, his hands imprisoned in handcuffs.

'I'm sorry, mademoiselle,' said the inspector as he got to his feet. 'It's all over . . . I have a taxi at the door waiting for you . . . Radek and I still have lots to say to each other.'

The Czech sat up, incandescent, wild-eyed. Maigret laid one heavy hand on his shoulder and said:

'Now isn't that so, little man!'

11. Four Aces

From 3 a.m. to dawn, light shone in Maigret's office on Quai des Orfèvres, and the few police officers who had work to do in the building could hear the dull drone of voices.

At eight, the inspector sent the office clerk to bring up two breakfasts. Then he phoned Coméliau, the examining magistrate, at his home.

It was nine o'clock when the door opened. Maigret emerged behind Radek, who was no longer hand-cuffed.

Both men looked equally exhausted. But neither murderer nor inquisitor displayed any sign of animosity.

'Is it this way?' asked the Czech when they reached the end of a corridor.

'Yes. We'll go through the Palais de Justice. It will be quicker . . .'

He led him through the passage to Paris' central police station reserved for members of the Préfecture, to be booked. The formalities did not take long. As a guard escorted Radek to the cells, Maigret gave him a look, as if he were about to say something, perhaps goodbye, but instead he shrugged his shoulders and made his way slowly to Monsieur Coméliau's office.

*

The magistrate was on the defensive and, when there was a knock at the door, he adopted an air of casual unconcern. But there was no need.

Maigret did not crow. He did not gloat, nor were his words sarcastic. He just looked haggard, like a man who has just completed a long and arduous task.

'Mind if I smoke? . . . Thanks . . . It's cold in here . . .'

And he directed a bilious look at the central heating, which had been removed from his own office at his orders and replaced by an old cast-iron stove.

'It's all over . . . As I told you over the phone, he has confessed . . . I don't think you'll have any more problems with him. He's a good loser and concedes that he's lost the game.'

The inspector had made notes on scraps of paper, which he would need to write up his report, but he had mixed them up and now stuffed them back in his pocket with a sigh.

'The distinguishing feature of this case . . .' he began.

But the expression was far too high-flown for him. He got to his feet and began pacing up and down with his hands clasped behind his back. Then he resumed:

'This case was a frame-up from the start! That's the top and bottom of it! It's not my word but the murderer's. And even when he said it, the murderer himself did not appreciate the full extent of what he was saying.

'What struck me when Joseph Heurtin was arrested was that it was not possible to slot his crime into any category. He did not know the victim. He hadn't stolen anything. He had no sadistic tendencies and he wasn't deranged.

'I wanted to review the investigation and I found that all the evidence had an increasingly false ring to it.

'And false is, I assure you, the right word. Not accidentally false but knowingly, even scientifically, false! False in ways designed to mislead the police and direct the courts towards the most disastrous of outcomes!

'And what can be said about the real murderer? That he is even more false than the whole of his carefully staged plot.

'You know as well as I do the workings of the minds of different sorts of criminals.

'Well, neither of us could know what went on in the mind of someone like Radek.

'I've stayed close to him for the last week, watching him, trying to guess what he was thinking. A week of going from one staggering discovery to another, a week of being led up the garden path!

'He has a cast of mind which defeats all our attempts at classification! Which is why he would never have been involved in our inquiries at all *if he hadn't had some obscure desire to be caught*!

'Because it was he who gave me the leads I needed. And he did it with a confused sense that he was risking his own downfall . . . And yet he just carried on.

'And what if I told you that he now seems more relieved than anything else . . . ?'

Maigret had not raised his voice. But there was a controlled intensity about him which gave his words extraordinary power. From outside came the sound of comings and goings in the corridors of the prosecutor's office, and at intervals a court usher would call a name, or gendarmes would tramp by in their boots.

'A man who has killed, not with a particular object in mind, but for killing's sake! I almost said, for fun . . . No, don't object . . . You'll see . . . I shouldn't think he'll talk much, or even answer the questions you put to him, because he's told me that all he wants now is one thing: peace.

'But the evidence which will be supplied to you will be enough.

'His mother was a domestic servant in a small town in Czechoslovakia. He was brought up in a house in the suburbs which resembled an army barracks. And if he got himself an education it was because he was given scholarships and received support from charities.

'I'm certain that as a boy he was permanently scarred by his situation and that he started to hate the world, which he saw only from below.

'He was also a boy when he became convinced that he was a genius. To become famous and rich through his intelligence, that was the dream which brought him to Paris, where he had to accept that his mother, who was sixty-five years of age and suffering from a disease of the marrow of her spinal column, was still working as a servant so that she could send him money!

'His pride was inordinate, all-consuming! And it was compounded by impatience, for Radek, a medical student, knew that he was suffering from the same disease as his mother and that he had only a few years to live.

'At the outset, he worked like a slave, and his teachers were amazed by his ability.

'He made no friends and did not talk to anyone. He was poor, but he was used to poverty.

'He often attended lectures wearing nothing at all on his feet. At various times, he unloaded vegetables at the market at Les Halles to earn a little money.

'But this did not prevent the inevitable happening. His mother died. The money stopped coming.

'Then suddenly, from one day to the next, he abandoned his dreams. He could have worked, as many students do. But he didn't even try. Did he suspect that he would never be the man of genius he had always wanted to be? Did he doubt himself?

'So he did nothing. *Absolutely nothing!* He hung around brasseries. He wrote letters to distant relatives asking for financial support. He got money from charitable organizations. He scrounged off fellow countrymen, cynically, even making a virtue of his lack of gratitude.

'The world did not understand him! So he hated the world!

'He spent all his time nurturing his hatred. In Montparnasse, he sat next to people who were happy, rich and healthy. He drank café au lait while cocktails circulated at nearby tables.

'Did he think of turning to crime? Perhaps. Twenty years ago, he would have become a militant anarchist, and you'd have found him throwing a bomb in a capital city somewhere. But that's no longer the fashion.

'He was alone and wanted to remain apart. He brooded. He took a perverse pleasure in being alone, in the knowledge of his own superiority and of the unfairness of fate towards him.

'He was remarkably intelligent but had an even more acute sense of human weakness.

'One of his professors told me about a strange compulsion he already had at medical school which made him quite frightening. He had only to observe someone for a few minutes and he would be able to *sense* that person's physical defects.

'Once he gleefully told a young man who was not expecting it:

'"Three years from now you'll be in a sanatorium!"

'Or:

'"Your father died of cancer, didn't he! So you take care!"

'Such accurate diagnostic ability was unheard of! And it applied to both inherited physical and mental conditions.

'It was his only form of entertainment as he sat in his corner at the Coupole. He was sick himself and was always watching out for signs of sickness in others.

'Crosby came within his observational ambit, for he was a regular at the same bar. Radek painted me a picture of him which was strikingly true.

'Where, I admit, I had seen only what we would call a daddy's boy, no more, a fairly run-of-the-mill playboy, Radek showed the cracks in the façade.

'He described a Crosby who was fit and well, popular with women, enjoying life to the full, but also a Crosby who was prepared to do the most appalling things to satisfy his desires.

'A Crosby who for a whole year allowed his wife to remain on the friendliest terms with his mistress, Edna Reichberg, while all the time knowing that at the first opportunity he would get a divorce so that he could marry the girl.

'A Crosby who, one evening, when both women had just left him to go to the theatre, allowed his frustrations to appear all over his face.

'It happened at the Coupole, at a table at the far end of the room. He was with a couple of friends who were indistinguishable from the many others he had. He said with a sigh:

'"To think that just yesterday some moron killed an old woman who ran a shop for twenty-two francs! Me, I'd willingly give a hundred thousand to someone who would get rid my aunt for me!"

'Was he joking? Exaggerating? Was it wishful thinking?

'Radek was there. He hated Crosby more than the rest because he was the most glittering of the people he came into contact with.

'The Czech knew Crosby better than Crosby knew himself. And Crosby had never even noticed him!

'He got to his feet. In the gents' cloakroom he scribbled on a piece of paper:

'*Agree price of 100,000. Send key addressed to initials M. V., poste restante, Boulevard Raspail.*

'He went back to his table. A waiter delivered the note to Crosby, who gave a mocking laugh then went on with his conversation, though not without looking round at all the customers nearby.

'A quarter of an hour later, Mrs Henderson's nephew asked the waiter to bring the poker dice.

'"Playing all by yourself?" joked one of his companions.

'"Just an idea . . . I want to know if I can roll at least two aces with my first go."

'"And if you do it?"

'"Then the answer's *yes*."

'"*Yes* to what?"

'"Just an idea. Don't worry."

'And he shook the dice round and round in the cup for a long time then with a trembling hand rolled them.

'"Four aces!"

'He wiped the sweat off his forehead, got up and left, after making a joke which sounded hollow. The next evening, the key was sent to Radek.'

Eventually, Maigret sat down heavily on a chair, straddling it as he usually did.

'It was Radek who told me about the episode of the four aces. I'm convinced that it's true and that Janvier, whom I've sent out to do something for me, will confirm it when he gets back in an hour or two. The rest, which I shall now tell you, as I have already told what went before, I put together piece by piece, fragment by fragment, while the Czech, whom I was tailing, unknowingly supplied me with new avenues to explore.

'Picture it. Radek has the key. He is less eager to get his

hands on the hundred thousand than to vent his hatred of the world.

'Crosby, envied or admired by all, is in his power. He's got him! He feels strong!

'Don't forget that Radek had nothing to expect from life. He was not even sure that he could hold out until his sickness swept him away. Perhaps he would be reduced to jumping in the Seine one night when he no longer had enough small change to pay for his café au lait.

'He was nothing! He had absolutely nothing to live for!

'I said just now that twenty years ago he would have been an anarchist. Nowadays, surrounded by the excitable, slightly unhinged denizens of Montparnasse, he found it far more amusing to pull off *a perfect crime*!

'A perfect crime. He was just a poor, sick nobody. And the papers would be full of an exploit of his! The wheels of the judicial machinery would start turning at a sign from him! A woman would die! A man like Crosby would quake in his boots!

'And he would be the only one in the know as he sat there with his usual café au lait, the only one to savour his power!

'There was just one indispensable condition: that he must not get caught. And to do that, the safest way would be to feed an innocent man into the great maw of Justice!

'He met Heurtin one evening on a café terrace. He studied him as he studied everybody. He spoke to him . . .

'Heurtin was just as much a fish out of water as Radek. He could have led a quiet life in his parents' inn. In Paris, a delivery man on 600 francs a month, he was unhappy and found escape in daydreams. He devoured cheap novels, went to the cinema regularly and imagined himself as the hero of marvellous adventures.

'He had no drive, nothing to protect him against the power of the Czech.

'"Would you like to earn in one night, with no risk to you, enough for you to live in whatever way you wanted?"

'Heurtin's heart beat faster. Radek had him! Radek revelled in his power and persuaded his new friend to accept the idea of a break-in.

'"Just a spot of burglary. The house is unoccupied!"

'He drew up a plan, anticipated everything his accomplice would do, every move he would make. It was his idea that he should buy a pair of shoes with rubber soles because, he said, they wouldn't make a noise. In reality, it was because he could then be sure that Heurtin would leave clear evidence that he had been there.

'It must have been an intoxicating time for Radek. He who didn't have the price of an aperitif – did he not feel omnipotent?

'And every day he rubbed shoulders with Crosby, who did not know him and found the wait unnerving.

'What led me to discover the truth about the events at the villa at Saint-Cloud, you know, was one sentence in the medical report. We never read the specialists' reports carefully enough. It was only four days ago that one detail struck me.

'The pathologist had written:

'*Some minutes after death, the body of Madame Henderson, which must have been lying on the very edge of the bed, rolled on to the floor.*

'Now you will concede that there was no reason why the murderer, several minutes after the crime, should touch the body on which there were no jewels or anything except a night-dress.

'But I return to the series of events. Radek confirmed them last night.

'He persuaded Heurtin to break into the villa at *exactly* 2.30 a.m., to go up to the first floor and enter the bedroom, all without turning any lights on. He swore to him that there was nobody in the house. And the place he said the valuables would be was where the bed was located.

'At 2.20 a.m., Radek, alone, killed both women, hid the knife in the wardrobe and left. Then he kept an eye out for Heurtin to show up. Heurtin carried out his instructions to the letter.

'Heurtin, groping in the dark, knocked the body on to the floor, panicked, switched a light on, saw the corpses, checked to see that they were really dead and left bloody fingerprints all over the place.

'When he finally made off, quaking in his boots, he ran into Radek, who behaved very differently, sneering at him and treating him cruelly.

'The meeting between the two of them must have been quite something. But what could a simple soul like Heurtin do against a man like Radek?

'He didn't even know the man's name or where he lived.

'The Czech showed him his rubber gloves and the over-shoes which meant that he had left no trace in the house.

'"You'll go down for this! Who's going to believe you? *No one will believe you!* And then you'll be executed!"

'A taxi was waiting for them on the opposite side of the Seine, at Boulogne. Radek did not stop talking.

'"If you keep your mouth shut, I'll save you! Do you understand? I'll get you out of jail, maybe in a month, maybe three. *But out you will get!*"

'Two days later, Heurtin, now under arrest, said nothing except to repeat that he hadn't killed anybody. He was in a state of shock. He told his mother about Radek, and only her.

'*But his mother didn't believe him!* Wasn't that the best proof that the other man was right, that the best thing to do was say nothing and wait for the promised help?

'Months passed. In his cell, Heurtin was haunted by the two dead bodies whose sticky blood he had felt on his hands. His only doubts came on the night when he heard the footsteps of the party of men who came to take the prisoner in the next cell to his place of execution.

'Then, the last breath of defiance went out of him. His father had not answered any of his letters and had forbidden his mother and his sister to visit him. He was alone, locked up with a nightmare.

'And then out of the blue he got a note telling him he was going to escape. He followed the instructions, but did so half-heartedly, going through the motions, and once out in Paris he wandered around aimlessly, eventually found a bed to collapse on and at last slept in a place which was not High Surveillance, where only men in the shadow of the guillotine ever sleep.

'The next day, he suddenly found Inspector Dufour standing in front of him. Heurtin scented police and danger and instinctively hit out, got away and resumed his wandering.

'Freedom did not stop him thinking clearly. He knew exactly what to do. He had no money. No one was waiting for him.

'And all on account of Radek! He went looking for him in the cafés where they had first met.

'To kill him, perhaps? But he had no weapon, though he was sufficiently enraged to throttle him with his bare hands! Maybe also to ask him to bail him out, or just simply because he was the only person he could still speak to.

'He caught sight of him in the Coupole. They wouldn't let him in. So he waited. He walked up and down, like the village idiot, and sometimes pressed his white face against the window.

'When Radek finally emerged, it was between two policemen. Heurtin wandered off blindly, instinctively going to earth, back to the house at Nandy, where he was no longer welcome . . . He dropped on to a pile of hay, in an outhouse.

'And when his father gave him until nightfall to get out, he chose instead to hang himself.'

Maigret shrugged and growled:

'He'll never swim against the current again. Oh, he'll live but he'll be marked by what happened. Of all Radek's victims he is the most to be pitied.

'Yes, there were others, and there'd have been more if . . .

'But I'll tell you about them later . . . Once the crime

had been committed and Heurtin was behind bars, the Czech took up his life again, going from one café to the next. He did not ask Crosby for his hundred thousand francs, primarily because it wouldn't be a safe thing to do, or perhaps because his poverty had become necessary to him, since it stoked his hatred for mankind.

'At the Coupole he could observe the American, whose good humour was no longer quite as carefree. Crosby was waiting . . . He had never met the man who had written the note . . . He was convinced that Heurtin was guilty . . . But he was scared that Heurtin would give him away!

'But it never happened. The man charged with the crime allowed himself to be found guilty. There was talk that he would be executed soon, and then Madame Henderson's heir would be able to breathe easily again.

'What was going on in Radek's mind? He had pulled off his perfect crime. It had gone smoothly down to the very last detail. Nobody suspected him.

'It was what he had wanted: he was the only person in the entire world who knew the truth! And when he saw the Crosbys sitting round their table in the bar, he thought that one word from him would be enough to put the fear of God into them!

'And yet he wasn't satisfied. His life was still just as dull. Nothing had changed except that two women were dead, and a poor devil was about to have his head cut off.

'I couldn't swear to it, but I'd bet that what weighed most heavily on him was that he had no one to admire him. No one who'd murmur as he passed by:

'"He's not much to look at but he committed one of the

most perfect crimes imaginable! He outsmarted the police, fooled the courts and changed the course of several lives."

'It's something that's happened to other murderers. Most of them have felt the need to confide in somebody, even if it was only some tart they'd picked up.

'But Radek was above that. Anyway, he was never much interested in women.

'Then one morning the papers reported that Heurtin had escaped. Wasn't this the opportunity he'd been looking for? He decided to give the cards another shuffle and take an active part once more.

'He wrote to *Le Sifflet*. He took fright when he saw his erstwhile accomplice watching him and delivered himself up into the hands of the police . . . But what he wanted was admiration . . . He wanted to be known as a man who played a good hand.

'So he threw down the challenge: "You'll never understand anything!"

'From that moment on, it was all feverish excitement. He sensed that in the end he'd be arrested! Better still, it was in his power to bring that moment nearer! He deliberately committed compromising acts as if an inner force was urging him to want to seek punishment.

'He no longer had a role in life. He was doomed. Everything filled him with disgust or indignation . . . He was dragging out a mean, wretched existence.

'He knew that I would stay close to him, that I'd get there in the end . . .

'And then he developed a kind of neurosis . . . He showed off. He took satisfaction in pulling the wool over my eyes.

'Hadn't he got the better of Heurtin and Crosby? Wouldn't he get the better of me too?

'He made up things to confuse me. For example, he pointed out that all the events connected with the case had taken place not far from the Seine.

'Surely I'd let myself be put off my stroke and get distracted by a false lead?

'He proceeded to multiply the false leads. He lived in a state of over-excitement. He was finished but he still went on fighting, playing games with life.

'Why didn't he make a start by bringing Crosby down with him?

'He had constructed an image for himself as all-powerful, a demi-god. He phoned Crosby and demanded his hundred thousand francs.

'He showed me the money. He felt an unholy glee juggling with his freedom in this way.

'It was he who made Crosby go out to the villa at Saint-Cloud at a given time. Now that was typical in psychological terms. He had seen me a little earlier. He realized that I had decided to reopen the investigation, starting again from square one.

'It followed that I'd go out to Saint-Cloud – and find Crosby, who would have some difficulty explaining his presence there.

'Did he anticipate that the man who now believed that his secret was out would kill himself? It's possible. Even probable.

'But it wasn't enough for him. He became more and more intoxicated with his own power.

'And it was because I sensed that he was getting more and more out of control that I decided to stay with him, not saying much and being dour. I was always there, morning to night, night to morning.

'Would his nerve hold? A number of small things told me that he was on a dangerously slippery slope. He felt a constant need to feed his hatred of the world. He humiliated children, made cruel fun of a beggar woman, incited tarts to scratch each other's eyes out . . .

'And he tried to work out what effect it was all having on me. He was play-acting all the time!

'It couldn't be long now before he fell flat on his face. The way things were, he wouldn't maintain his self-control for much longer . . . It was inevitable that he would make a mistake.

'And he did! All great criminals invariably do, sooner or later.

'He had killed two women! He had killed Crosby! He had turned Heurtin into a human wreck . . .

'He would go on with the carnage until the very end.

'But I took certain precautions. I sent Janvier to the Georges V to get hold of all letters addressed to Madame Crosby and Edna Reichberg and intercept all their phone calls.

'I never left Radek by himself, but on two occasions he gave me the slip for a few minutes, and I guessed that he had been posting letters.

'A few hours later, Janvier would hand them to me. Here they are. One of them informed Madame Crosby that her husband had arranged for Madame Henderson to be murdered. Enclosed with it, as proof, was the box containing the key: the address on it was written in her husband's hand.

'Radek knew the law. His letter pointed out that a murderer cannot be the heir of his victim, and that therefore Madame Crosby would have to surrender all the money.

'He ordered her to go at midnight to the Citanguette and search in the mattress in one of the rooms for the knife which was used in the murder and to hide it in a safe place.

'If the weapon was not there, she was to go to Saint-Cloud and look for it in a wardrobe.

'You will again note this need to humiliate people as well as to muddy the waters. Madame Crosby drew a blank at the Citanguette for the good reason that the knife was never there.

'But it gave Radek enormous satisfaction to send a rich American woman into a hang-out for tramps.

'But that's not all. His mania for complicating things went much deeper. He told Madame Crosby that Edna Reichberg was the mistress of her husband who intended to marry her.

'*She knows the full story,* he'd written to Crosby's widow. *She hates you and if she gets the chance she'll blab what she knows because she wants to reduce you to poverty.*'

Maigret wiped his brow and sighed.

'How idiotic! That's what you're thinking, isn't it! It was like a nightmare. But don't forget that for years Radek had spent his waking hours dreaming of such exquisite moments of revenge.

'Actually, his calculation was not far out. A second letter to Edna Reichberg stated that Crosby was the murderer, and that proof of his guilt would be found in the wardrobe. It added that she could avoid a scandal by retrieving the weapon from it at a set time.

'He added that from the start Madame Crosby had known all about her husband's crime.

'As I've already said, he had come to regard himself as a demigod.

'The two letters never reached the persons they were intended for for the simple reason that Janvier brought them to me.

'But how was I to prove that Radek had sent them? Like the note sent to *Le Sifflet*, they had been written with the left hand.

'I then invited both women to take part in an experiment, explaining that it would help us find the man who had killed Madame Henderson.

'I told them to follow the instructions in Radek's letters exactly.

'Radek himself led me to the Citanguette and from there to Saint-Cloud.

'Did he have a feeling that this was the end of the road? And a magnificent climax it would have been – if his letters had not been intercepted!

'The theory was that Madame Crosby, frightened by the murderer's revelations and still smarting from her experience at the Citanguette, would drive out to the villa at Saint-Cloud and make straight for the bedroom where the double murder had been committed.

'Imagine the state of her nerves! She would find herself confronted by Edna Reichberg who would be holding the knife!

'I wouldn't like to say if the encounter would have ended in murder. But I am inclined to think that in psychological terms Radek was not all that wide of the mark . . .

'The events set in train by me worked out differently. Madame Crosby left the villa alone.

'Radek was racked by the need to know what she had done with Edna.

'He followed me upstairs . . . It was he who opened the wardrobe door. Inside, he found, not a corpse, but the Swedish girl alive and well.

'He stared at me . . . He *knew* . . .'

'And then he did the thing I had been expecting: *he pulled the trigger of his gun!*'

The examining magistrate opened his eyes wide.

'Don't worry. Earlier that afternoon, I had deliberately bumped into him and switched his loaded revolver for another one with an empty chamber. The game was over. He had played and he had lost!'

Maigret refilled his pipe which had gone out and then stood up, his forehead furrowed like a five-barred gate.

'I would add that he was a good loser . . . We spent the rest of the night together at Quai des Orfèvres . . . I was honest with him, told him all I knew, and, though at first he enjoyed himself laying false trails, he gave up playing games after less than an hour.

'After that he filled in the gaps, with just a touch of bravado.

'He is now surprisingly calm. He asked if I thought he would be executed. And when I hesitated with my answer, he added with a sneer:

'"Do your damnedest, inspector, to ensure that I am. You owe me a small favour. You see, I've got this idea. Once I was present at an execution in Germany. Until the very last moment, the prisoner, who had shown no emotion, started yelling and calling for his mother. I'd be curious to find out if I'd call for my mother too! What do you reckon?"'

Both men fell silent. The sounds of the Palais de Justice were more distinct now, and they came against a background of the muffled rumble of Paris.

After a time, Monsieur Coméliau pushed aside the file which, at the start of the interview, for appearances, he had opened in front of him.

'Very well, detective chief inspector,' he began. 'I . . .'

His eyes were elsewhere. Pink patches glowed around his cheek bones.

'I'd be grateful if you'd forget the . . . er . . .'

But as he began putting on his overcoat, Maigret held out his hand. It was the most natural thing in the world.

'You'll have my report tomorrow. But now, I must go and see Moers. I promised to let him have the two letters. He's thinking of doing a full graphological study of them.'

After a moment's hesitation, he walked to the door but turned round and had a sight of the magistrate's mortified expression, then he was gone. On his face was a faint, lingering smile which was his only revenge.

12. The Fall

The month was January. There had been a frost. The ten men who were there had the collars of their overcoats turned up and their hands sunk deep in their pockets.

Most exchanged disjointed comments as they stamped their feet to keep warm and kept shooting furtive glances all in the same direction.

Only Maigret stood apart, his neck sunk into his shoulders, and his mood so foul that no one had dared speak to him.

In the nearby apartment blocks there were lights in a few of the windows, for dawn was only just breaking. From somewhere came the tinny clatter of trams.

And then there was the noise of a car, a door slammed, then the sound of heavy shoes and of orders issued in a hushed voice.

A reporter took notes. He looked uneasy. A man turned his head away.

Radek stepped lightly out of the police van and looked around him. His eyes were clear and on them, in the morning greyness, were the infinite reflections of the oceans.

He was being held on both sides. It did not bother him, and he strode out vigorously in the direction of the scaffold.

As he did so, he slipped on the ice and fell. His guards,

167

thinking that he was trying to escape, rushed in and held him down.

It lasted only seconds. But perhaps this fall was the most painful thing of all: painful, indeed, was the shamed expression on the condemned man's face when he regained his feet, having lost all the bounce and confidence with which he had primed himself.

His eye fell on Maigret, whom he had asked to be present at his execution.

The inspector tried to avoid his gaze.

'So you came, then . . .'

Some of the men were getting restive, nerves were on edge, fretting with the same distressing urge to have it all over and done with.

Radek turned to look at the patch of ice and with a sardonic smile motioned to the scaffold and said mockingly:

'That was a close shave!'

There was a momentary hesitation on the part of the men who had been charged with ending a man's life.

One of them said something. A car horn blared in a street close by.

It was Radek, without a glance for anyone, who was first to step forward.

'Inspector . . .'

One minute more perhaps and it would all be over. The voice had an odd sound to it.

'I expect you'll be going straight home to your wife, right? She'll have coffee ready . . .'

Maigret saw no more, heard nothing else. It was true.

His wife was waiting for him in their warm dining room, where they always had breakfast.

Without knowing why, he did not have the courage to go home. He went directly to Quai des Orfèvres, filled the stove in his office to the top and poked it so hard that he very nearly broke the bars.

INSPECTOR MAIGRET

OTHER TITLES IN THIS SERIES

And more to follow

www.penguin.com